THE WOMAN WAS A VICIOUS GOSSIP.

And Sarah had given her a sharp set-down, a display of rudeness that she feared would not be taken lightly by society. Why had she done it?

True, she had been blinded by anger, but, she had to admit, more by her fierce determination to stand by Ravenwilde in the face of the unwarranted slander uttered by Lady Waxton. But what if the slander had been *warranted*? Would she still have stood by him? YES... YES... YES...! her heart screamed. In the darkness of the night and of her own despair, Sarah was forced to admit that she had thrown discretion to the winds because she had fallen in love with Duke of Ravenwilde.

FINAL SEASON

Edna Maye Manley

FAWCETT COVENTRY • NEW YORK

A Fawcett Coventry Book
Published by Ballantine Books
Copyright © 1982 by Edna Maye Manley

ISBN 0-449-50306-2

Manufactured in the United States of America

First Ballantine Books Edition: August 1982

Chapter 1

Although Miss Sarah Windemere took with her a basket ordinarily used for gathering blueberries, it was merely for purposes of camouflage. She might indeed pick a few berries if any should come her way, but she was in fact in search of nothing more than peace and quiet. Since announcing her intentions over a week past of removing herself from her sister's home, or to be more exact, her brother-in-law's home, to set up an establishment of her own, Lady Sandover had made life all but insupportable for Sarah.

"But my dear Sarah," Lady Sandover had objected again that very morning, using failing accents and reclining in the blue parlor while hugging to her breast the bad-tempered pug who was never far from her person, "you simply cannot do such a thing as set up your own establishment. Whatever will people say? Dear Randolph and I will be the talk of the neighborhood, and London as well when the season gets under way."

Even if Sarah had been inclined to give her opinion as to what people might say, which she was not, her sister gave her no opportunity but proceeded to answer her own question. "I'll tell you what they will say. They will say that dear Randolph and I pushed you out, or at least that we are so unfeeling as not to care what you do and what becomes of you. No, my dear, I simply cannot allow it."

Judith rarely raised her voice but expressed her opinions and wishes in softly spoken tones which managed to suggest that if they were not agreed to, there would result dire consequences either for herself or, more likely, for the person who was so unwise as to disagree with her. Consequently, her tyranny over her servants, other members of the family, and even her husband was complete. No one wanted that lady's illness, or even death, laid at *his* door, and even less did he want to feel the sharp edge of her tongue.

However, Sarah was made of sterner stuff. "I'm sorry, Ju," she began.

Lady Sandover had not given up hopes of whipping Sarah into line, and she interrupted her to say with a pained expression, "Please don't call me Ju. How many times must I ask you not to call me that? Really, Sarah, we both of us have long since outgrown such childish names, and I believe our respective stations demand more formality, even between sisters."

"I'm sorry, *Judith*," Sarah answered, barely concealing the twitch at the corners of her generous mouth. Most of the time she was vastly amused at the self-important consequences her sister had acquired since marrying the very eligible Lord Sandover, and so she was now, but just lately she had become more and more annoyed and at times found her usual good spirits sinking very low indeed, surrounded as she was by a total lack of humor or mirth. "Truly, I'm sorry to disoblige you, but I surely don't have to remind you that you have no authority over my actions. You can neither allow nor disallow anything I want to do."

"No," Judith agreed reluctantly, "I don't have any authority in any *legal* sense, but I do have a *moral* obligation and a *duty* to the family to consider. I can't imagine what Papa was thinking when he left his will in such a way as to make you sole mistress of your fortune. Any father with the least bit of forethought would have made dear Randolph your guardian and trustee until such time as you acquired a husband of your own to manage for you."

It was a complaint which Sarah had heard many times, and each time she heard it, she blessed her departed parent a thousand times over. As to why he had seen to it before his death that she would be independent, Sarah could only surmise that being a man of humor, sensitivity, and perception (qualities which Judith could neither recognize nor appreciate), he had concluded early in his relationship with his esteemed son-in-law that to leave his only daughter dependent upon a man (however worthy) who was totally lacking in humor and so greatly impressed with his own consequence would be to do her a great disservice and, for a girl with Sarah's spirit and disposition, would amount to no less than criminal folly.

"Papa has left you prey to every fortune hunter in the country," Judith continued to bemoan while trying to calm the pug, who was taking exception—in the form of low growls and much agitation of movement—to the heightened emotions he sensed in his mistress. "God alone knows what will become of you if you leave the protection of dear Randolph's home and influence."

"Well," Sarah answered rashly. "I certainly haven't yet succumbed to the charms of any of the fortune hunters your husband has so far brought my way." Too late she realized she had fallen into another of Judith's verbal traps.

"Now, that remark is ungrateful and unworthy as well as untrue," Judith chided gently. She had the satisfaction of seeing Sarah flush uncomfortably. "Dear Randolph has brought you to the attention of any number of his friends in the hope of effecting a suitable marriage for you. How you can possibly refer to any of those most worthy gentlemen as fortune hunters, I can't imagine." She continued to press home her advantage. "I'm sorry to say, dear Sarah, that your character is shockingly lacking in the finer attributes that a lady of your breeding and upbringing should possess. You lean far too much to levity and the frivolous. A perfect example is your shocking behavior on the occasion when Sir Laxall paid you the honor of asking your hand in marriage. We found you positively bent over in laughter after the poor man left."

Far from reducing Sarah to greater depths of discomfiture, as Judith had hoped, the memory of Sir Laxall on one knee, his stays creaking and his face red and perspiring from the effort of contorting his rotund body into such an uncomfortable and ridiculous position, restored a decided twinkle to her fine gray eyes. She had thought at the time, and truth to tell still thought, that she had admirably concealed her vast amusement, saying all that was proper for a young lady to say when declining an offer of marriage. Why, there had been only the barest twinge at the corners of her mouth until the gentleman was well out of hearing. Naturally she had been able to contain herself no longer than was necessary and had indeed been doubled over with laughter, tears streaming down her face and arms clutching her aching sides, when her sister and brother-in-law had come to see what her answer had been.

"If you will but consider the vast proportions of the gentleman's person, Judith, I think that even you must admit to the ridiculous figure Sir Laxall made of himself. No, really, dear sister, I cannot persuade myself to feel the least tendre for a hideously fat man, no matter how great may be his consequence," Sarah answered with only a slight quiver in her voice.

While Judith might privately agree that the gentleman was indeed much too fat to be pleasing, she continued to complain that Sarah was perhaps a trifle too nice in her expectations and informed her that many happy marriages had been achieved between ladies and gentlemen who had far less in common than Sarah had with more than one of the gentlemen who had done her the honor of paying their addresses to her, not to mention those whom Sarah had been so unwise as to hint off before they had come to the sticking point (a phrase which Sarah found vulgar in the extreme, and her finely arched brows rose in some surprise at hearing her very proper sister utter it). While Judith gave her advice on the proper way for a gently bred lady to comport herself, Sarah allowed her mind to wander, barely hearing the droning of her sister's voice.

Judith could not quite believe that Sarah was serious in her determination to set up her own establishment, but Sarah, thanks to her father's generosity and foresight, was the sole owner of a lovely house in Brook Street in London as well as Foxborough, a small but neat establishment that had once been a hunting box but had, over the years, been added to and remodeled. It was situated in Northampton, not many miles from the family estate and a mere day's journey from London. Sarah was determined to escape (there was no other word she felt described her removal from her present abode) and live her own life.

She was far more aware of the restrictions society placed on ladies of her birth than Judith appeared to realize, and she had no intentions of flying in the face of these restrictions. It was never her desire to behave in any way that would bring the least criticism or censure upon either herself or her family name. However, she was also aware that having reached the age of seven and twenty, many of the restrictions which would attend a green girl just out of the schoolroom and making her first bow to society did not apply to her any more. Indeed, everyone except members of her immediate family considered her to be on the shelf, and fond mamas no longer saw her as a threat to their daughters chances among the eligible gentlemen of the ton.

Of course, she still had a respectable court of admirers, but even she recognized that it was of late made up mostly of older gentlemen, widowers with children who needed a mother, perennial flirts who now considered her old enough to understand the rules of the game and not expect an offer of marriage to follow gallant attentions, and not a few very young bucks who were just down from Oxford and fancied themselves to be in love, or at least half in love, with an "older woman."

There were also at least three gentlemen, unexceptionable in every way, who still dangled after her and would, with just the slightest encouragement, make an offer. Although these gentlemen would be considered good matches, and indeed one of them would be called a brilliant match, Sarah found herself unable to feel more than a friendly interest in any one of the three. She had gone over in her mind any number of times the virtues of each and the advantages she herself would enjoy should she form an alliance with any one of them, but none of the advantages could outweigh the fact that she would be entering into a loveless marriage and be tied for the rest of her life to a man for whom she could feel only mild affection and respect. She had marveled with a wry sense of humor at how many toads she had encountered without once meeting Prince Charming.

Not that she was actually looking for a Prince Charming. She was of far too practical a mind (in spite of what Ju might say) to expect such a thing to happen outside the romances one found at the lending library. However, surely one could expect love to enter into a condition as intimate and lasting as marriage, and she had determined long ago, even before her father's death, that she would not enter into a marriage of convenience. It seemed to her that marriages of convenience were too often convenient for everyone except the parties most personally involved, and since her father had left her most comfortably situated, she saw no reason to make herself *uncomfortable* simply because it was expected of a young lady in her circumstances to marry.

"Sarah, are you attending me?" Judith asked sharply, penetrating Sarah's wandering thoughts.

"I'm sorry, Ju...ah, Judith. I'm afraid I was wool-gathering. What did you say?" If she was truly sorry, her tone did not betray it, as Judith was quick to point out.

"Well, I am most certainly attending you now," Sarah responded. "What was it you wished to ask me?"

"I was *asking* you nothing. I was merely pointing out to you that Mr. Brooks is reported to have at least thirty thousand a year, not to mention his vast estates and the house in Grosvenor Square, and a gentleman with that kind of wealth is not contemptible."

"Certainly not," Sarah replied, "and, indeed, if he were possessed of a mere competence, Mr. Brooks would not be a man to hold in contempt. He is most unexceptionable in every way. He is not unhandsome, his manners are very pleasing, and he always comports himself just as he ought."

"Well," Judith purred, "I had no idea you held him in such high esteem. Does this mean that you are beginning to consider his suit with favor? I can hardly wait to tell dear Randolph. How pleased he will be!"

"Certainly not!" Sarah answered sharply. "I have no intention of marrying Mr. Brooks. I was merely agreeing with you that he is not contemptible."

"But if you recognize all his sterling qualities, how can you not look with favor upon his suit? You are a most unnatural girl, Sarah, and I worry that you will end up a positive quiz."

"You may be right, sister, but I will *not* end up unhappily married," Sarah answered. "In the first place, I cannot feel any more for Mr. Brooks than friendship, and in the second place, he is much too old for me, or else I am too young for him. He must be all of five and fifty." A definite sparkle was beginning to flash in Sarah's usually calm gray eyes, and even Judith recognized and had a healthy respect for Sarah's anger.

"Very well," Judith relented, "just leave me for now. I feel one of my megrims coming on. We'll discuss this later. Dear Randolph will have something to say to you also, but until then, please go. Send Molly to me so that she might massage my brow with lavender water."

After seeking out Judith's maid and giving her Judith's instructions, Sarah went through the kitchens, found the basket for blueberries, and, making a wide detour of the stables for fear of meeting with Lord Sandover, who was wont to add his protests to those of his lady, came by a roundabout way to the kennels, where she requested of the keeper that he bring around her spaniel pup.

Casper, as Sarah had christened the pup, was inordinately pleased to see his mistress and at once began straining at the leash and jumping up to place his enormous (for such a small dog) muddy paws on the skirt of her fresh sprig muslin gown.

"I'm right sorry, Miss Sarah," Ned said sadly. "I've tried, 'deed I have, but the pup just won't take to training."

"Never mind, Ned," Sarah answered, bestowing upon him a dazzling smile. "I'm sure it isn't your fault."

"No, ma'am," he agreed. "Now they's some mighty fine, well-behaved pups came out of that same litter. Why don't you swap him for another?"

"Oh, no! Casper and I deal very well together. And besides, what would become of him?"

It was a rhetorical question; they both knew he would be drowned in the meadow pond. Such was the fate of dogs that would not conform.

When they were out of Ned's sight and hearing, Sarah removed the leash to let the pup run free. As he licked her hands in gratitude, she said wryly, "I expect my sister is wishing she could dispose of me in the same manner. Well, we'll neither of us be drowned nor leashed for life, my love."

Casper heartily approved his mistress's resolve and began wagging his tail and jumping up and down around her skirts, often losing his balance and rolling in the grass.

"Come along, you silly pup," Sarah laughed. "Let us get away from sight of the house as quickly as we can. We shall have the whole of the afternoon free from our leashes if we hurry away before someone sees us and decides to call us back.

"I shall take you up to London with me next week," Sarah promised the pup as he cavorted around her legs. "I'm sure the servants there will be kind to you. They were always kind to me."

By this time they had left the manicured grounds of Lord Randolph's estate and entered the woods close by. Sarah had no hesitation in walking in these woods, for she knew they belonged to her brother-in-law and there were some well-defined paths for her and the pup to enjoy. She often came here when the atmosphere at the house became too heavy for her to bear with equanimity.

Sitting down in a cleared, grassy spot, she took the pup onto her lap and continued to burden his willing ears with gentle complaints which were mixed with wry humor.

"You know, love, I can't decide whom I dislike most in that household. Sometimes I think it's that miserable pug Judith insists upon hugging to her bosom. She barely puts him down long enough to eat her meals. But just when I think *him* the most odious creature in all of England with his bad manners and worse temper, along comes Charles, who, at the tender age of ten summers, is already obnoxious to an unbelievable degree. I suppose I should feel sorry for the little wretch, for he grows more like his father every day, already full of conceit and self-importance. Do you know the little baggage had the effrontery to suggest to me yesterday that I was living in *his* house on *sufferance,* as though I were a poor relation? Let me tell you, Casper," Miss Windemere said with a great deal of asperity, which made poor Casper cower and cover his eyes with his great paws until Sarah assured him with gentle pats and kind words that she was not angry with him, "that I was very much tempted to box his ears for him. Then I remembered that the little beggar really can't help being what he is; just look at his mama and papa. Besides being pompous and self-righteous, Randolph is a *dead bore.* And Judith! Really, Casper, I know one should feel at least some slight affection for members of one's own family, but I *cannot* like her. I am persuaded that if I remain in that house above another sennight, I shall most certainly come to cuffs with her, and that really will not do. No, my pet, I think you and I should remove ourselves to London, and that just as soon as possible."

"All things considered," a male voice full of laughter said from the bushes directly behind Sarah, "I think you've made a wise decision."

Much astonished, Sarah rose to her feet with such haste that Casper was dumped unceremoniously onto the ground. Taking exception to such rough treatment and sensing the stranger to be the cause of it, he scrambled to his feet and greeted the gentleman emerging from the bushes leading a huge black horse with much barking and as ferocious a growl as one of his tender age could muster.

"Sit, and be quiet," the gentleman ordered the astonished Casper in a voice filled with more authority than he had yet encountered. Sarah watched with amazement as Casper sat back on his haunches so fast that he lost his balance and fell over on his back, where he remained while watching the gentleman with wary eyes.

If Casper's eyes were wary, Sarah's were not. Her lovely eyes, usually twinkling with good humor, were now a stormy gray. Her breast heaved with anger, and two bright-red spots appeared in her cheeks.

Addressing Casper, she said, "You miserable, ungrateful wretch! I shall have a great deal to say to *you* later," and turning to the gentleman who was the cause of her discomfiture, she stormed, "And you, sir, how dare you come upon us unannounced and begin giving orders to *my* dog?"

"Well, someone has to," the gentleman answered calmly. "He isn't very well behaved, is he?"

Sarah had to admit privately to the truth of this, but she was not about to retreat. "Perhaps not," she answered coldly, "but I fail to see what concern that can possibly be of yours. He is, after all, only a dog, and a puppy at that, but I should think a *gentleman* would know better than to eavesdrop on someone's private conversation."

"Well, yes," he admitted, amusement pouring from his soft brown eyes, "and so I do, but truth to tell, ma'am, I've never encountered a lady having a conversation, even a one-sided one, with a dog. Most people, you must admit, limit their communications with their dogs to 'sit,' or 'stay,' or 'come.'"

Sarah, who had always had a keen sense of and appreciation for the ridiculous, answered with a gurgling sound deep in her throat which soon gave way to a bubbling laugh. "Allright, sir, you win this round, but you must admit you are trespassing. I suppose you have a perfectly good explanation for that, also."

Laughter was still lurking in the depths of his eyes, but the gentleman answered with perfect solemnity. "Allow me to make myself known to you, ma'am," he said with a bow. I am Harry, Duke of Ravenwilde. My lands march with those of Lord Sandover. Actually, I've been out of the country for some years, and having returned just recently, I decided to call upon Lord Sandover. It seems our gamekeepers have been engaged in a running battle these past months, and I thought Lord Sandover and I might be able to settle the dispute before our respective servants shoot each other. My horse threw a shoe a short distance back, and while I was inspecting his foot and removing from it a stone he had picked up, you and your companion came by and began as charming a conversation as I have been honored to hear these many months."

"Well, I suppose that explains everything except why you did not immediately make yourself known to me," Sarah answered, somewhat placated by his explanation.

"Perhaps because I haven't been accustomed these past few years to adhering strictly to the dictates of good manners. One is inclined to become a trifle lax in these things living in India for extended periods of time," he answered with apparent honesty.

"No! Does one really? And have you been gone

from society for very long?" Sarah asked, very much interested and not in the least shocked by these revelations.

Now it was Ravenwilde's turn to laugh, and he did, throwing back his head and giving forth a full-bodied laugh which stretched his generous mouth even wider and exposed strong white teeth for Sarah's inspection. She was charmed, for she had not seen anyone laugh so since her father died.

While he continued to laugh, she took the opportunity to study him more closely. What she saw was a tall, well-built man in his late thirties or perhaps early forties. His black hair was worn a trifle shorter than fashion demanded and was liberally sprinkled with gray. His shoulders, encased in a coat of superfine cloth, were broad and his hips narrow. His legs were good and showed to advantage in buckskins and topboots. All in all, and in spite of (or perhaps because of?) the lines in his face, which she decided could just as well have been caused by dissipation as by the harsh climate of India, Sarah decided he was the most attractive man she had ever encountered.

When his mirth had subsided somewhat, Ravenwilde answered, "Yes, I've been gone for several years. You must still have been in the schoolroom when I left."

"Then you have indeed been gone a long time," Sarah answered in her candid fashion, "for you must know I am seven and twenty."

"No! Now why must I know that?" he answered with a decided twinkle in his eyes and a muscle twitching at the corners of his mouth.

Perceiving that his grace found this cause for amusement, Sarah said airly, "You, sir, may find cause to laugh at my advanced years, but I assure you my family does not."

"If I recollect the gentleman correctly, Lord Sandover finds little cause to laugh about *anything*. But perhaps age has mellowed him? Is he a relative of yours?"

"Not a *blood* relative," Sarah answered emphatically, which caused his grace to laugh out loud again.

"Ah, yes," he said, "I collect from your conversation with your noble companion that your sister— Judith, is it?—is married to Lord Sandover. That being so, she cannot be much like you. Do you have the same parents?" he asked curiously.

Rather than offending, this audacious question caused the bubbly laughter that so enchanted her admirers and angered her sister to surface as she answered, "Certainly! Poor Judith was not always so Friday-faced. It is just since she became engaged and married to Lord Sandover that she has lost her sense of humor. She is determined, you see, to live up to all his expectations, and as you have already indicated, you know him to be a man singularly lacking in humor. But really, sir, I have shown a shocking lack of deportment standing here in the woods talking to you thus. I really must leave you now."

"Really, must you? I had hoped you might walk with me back to the house and help me persuade someone in your stables to repair my horse's shoe while I call upon your brother-in-law," he answered on a pleading note.

"Well, of course, if you wish it. I only hope Judith does not see me until we are close to the house. She would be vastly shocked to see me emerging from the woods with you and would no doubt ring a peal over my head. And this time it would be *infinitely* worse than the others, for I find it lowering in the extreme to be *justly* chastised, don't you?"

Smiling warmly at her, Ravenwilde answered, "It has been many years since anyone has had the temerity to chastise me—justly or otherwise."

"Oh, how lovely that must be and how I do envy you your independent state. However, I suppose it must always be so with men. Women, even one of my advanced years, are hedged in on all sides by convention," Sarah answered wistfully.

"Do you then chafe against convention so much?" he asked, watching her closely.

"No, not really," she answered, furrowing her smooth brow. "It is just that everyone is so determined to see me married and I am equally determined not to marry until and unless my affections are engaged. Judith insists that I am foolish beyond permission to turn away so many eligible suitors," and having said this, she clapped her hand over her mouth and looked at him with stricken eyes. With color rushing to her face, she stammered, "Oh, dear, you must think me shockingly conceited. I never meant to imply that I am so very much sought after; actually only a very few..."

But his grace was again overcome by mirth, and when he could finally speak again he said, "Don't tease yourself so, my dear. If you are not positively inundated by suitors, the men in England must be excessively stupid. Surely things have not changed so much during my exile."

Blushing even more rosily at this compliment, Sarah declined to answer but instead began a minute study of the grass over which they were walking.

"You know, you are very lovely when you're shy and blushing, but I think I prefer you in a blazing anger." Before Sarah could reply to this, he continued, "No, actually, I like you best when you are at ease and speaking your mind so charmingly and candidly."

Very much discomfited by these outspoken observations, Sarah answered, "Sir, I fear I have given you a false impression of my character. Indeed, I was greatly at fault to engage in such easy conversation with any gentleman, much less one with whom I am not even acquainted. I do beg your pardon and ask that you forget what has taken place. My only excuse is that I have been blue deviled for so long that it was a great relief to meet someone with whom I could laugh."

He answered in a way that brought the faint blush back to her cheeks. "Surely shared laughter can be no bad thing; please allow me to laugh with you often."

"No, I suppose not," she answered hesitantly.

"And now, perhaps you will tell me your name?" he asked with a decided twinkle.

"Oh, goodness," she uttered with a gurgle of laughter. "Where are my manners? I, sir, am Miss Sarah Windemere."

"Miss Windemere," his grace answered with great seriousness as he bowed deeply, "I am your most obedient servant."

Affecting a deep curtsy, Sarah answered, "Sir, you are much too kind."

"Oh," he said seriously, "I am always kind to those of advanced years."

"Wretch," she said as they reached the stables, and seeing Lord Sandover riding up, she composed her features in readiness for the encounter.

"Randolph," she said as soon as he had handed over his horse to the groom, "I'm sure you remember your neighbor, the Duke of Ravenwilde. I met him on the path where his horse had thrown a shoe. He was on his way to meet with you, and I suggested that his horse might be attended to here in your stables while he conducted his business. I hope you will approve my actions."

Turning to Ravenwilde, she held out her hand and smiled innocently. "Thank you for your escort, sir. I'll leave you alone with Lord Sandover."

In an undertone which only she could hear, Ravenwilde said, "Little liar," and louder for Lord Sandover's benefit, "And thank you, Miss Windemere, for your directions. I look forward to meeting you again. Do you go to Lady Percivile's ball on Friday?"

"I'm afraid not, sir. You see, I depart for London in a week's time and will be very much occupied with the necessary arrangements. I believe my sister and brother-in-law mean to attend, however, and I'm sure you will enjoy their company. Goodbye, sir," and with that she walked away, very conscious of the twinkle that lurked in Ravenwilde's gentle brown eyes.

Chapter 2

After leaving Casper at the kennels, Sarah made her way to her own room without encountering her sister and stood gazing with unseeing eyes out the window. Whatever had possessed her to behave in so familiar a way with a perfect stranger? The fact that he had such frank and easy charm and address was no excuse for her to so far forget herself. A faint blush colored her ivory complexion as she remembered his compliments and decided that his manners were much too casual to be pleasing. Why, then, did they please her so much?

Sarah was no schoolroom miss to have her head turned by the compliments of an experienced man. She had seen several seasons and had engaged in any number of mild flirtations, but none had had quite the quality of this one. True, all her other flirtations had been conducted in strict propriety, while this time she had stood for quite half an hour or longer (where had the time gone?) alone in a secluded wood with a gentleman to whom she had never even been properly introduced. Perhaps, she told herself, that had lent a certain spice to the encounter which was lacking on a dance floor or at a respectable dinner party. Well, whatever the attraction, she sternly told herself, it must never happen again. This was just the sort of thing Judith would pounce upon to reinforce her argument that Sarah was not fit to set up her own establishment, and in her heart, Sarah knew she could not deny that she had acted most reprehensibly. What she should have done, of course, was immediately take her leave of the gentleman, but...

It had been such fun! And she had not had any fun for such a long time.

Convincing herself that if she should ever meet the gentleman again she would act with the strictest propriety, Sarah turned her attention to choosing a gown to wear for dinner and began her toilette without calling for the aid of her maid. She wanted to be alone for as long as possible and hug to herself the events of her never-to-be repeated afternoon.

However, she was not long left alone. There soon came a knock on her door, and Judith entered, hugging the despised pug to her breast. Recognizing the look on Judith's face, Sarah braced herself for what was to come.

"Well, Judith," she said lightly, "and how was your afternoon? Is the headache all gone?"

"Never mind *my* afternoon, it is *your* afternoon I'm interested in. Where did you meet Ravenwilde?" she demanded.

"Why, I told Randolph all about it," Sarah answered with as much nonchalance as she could muster. "We met on the path at the edge of the wood, where his horse threw a shoe. I accompanied him back to the stables, where we met Randolph. You must know he was coming to call upon Randolph to discuss some problem with regard to their respective gamekeepers. I assure you, sister, it was by the merest happenstance that he and I met."

"Randolph and I will not have you meeting with that *man*," Judith said with awful emphasis. "There is no one who is more likely to ruin your reputation. The man has no morals and no manners."

"Why, Judith," Sarah asked, astonished at the venom with which her sister denounced Ravenwilde, "whatever has the man done to incur such wrath? He seemed a pleasant enough sort to me the short time I was in his company."

With heaving breasts and flashing eyes, Judith answered, "Everyone knows the man for a gamester and a rakehell. His excesses were so great that he was instrumental in sending his father to an early grave. At one time he even so far forgot himself as to fight a duel over an actress. An *actress!* Can you imagine? There is no degradation to which he has not stooped, and finally, when he had run his course here in England, his father packed him off to India. It was said he would have cut his son out of his inheritance had it not been entailed. Not long after he left England, his father passed away and his stepmama refused even to notify him. There were those who were in a position to know who said that Ravenwilde even tried to seduce *her*, his own stepmama! She refused even to write to him when his father died, and when the lawyers finally located him, he refused to come home. Of course, he couldn't have gotten home in time for the burial, but one wonders if he would have come even if he could. They say there were many harsh words and hard feelings between Ravenwilde and his stepmama before he left, and you may be sure *he* was the cause of it. Why, just to be seen talking to him would be enough to compromise a young lady's reputation. That is why we forbid you to have anything further to do with him. Do I make myself clear, Sarah? As long as you enjoy the protection of our roof, you will steer clear of Ravenwilde."

As much as Sarah wanted to remind her sister that she was no longer a "young lady," a fact that Judith had been at great pains to make her aware of, and that she and Randolph had no right or authority to forbid her anything, and that as far as the protection of their roof was concerned, she, Sarah, could hardly wait to leave said protection behind her, she held her tongue. More than she wanted to give Judith the sharp set-down she so rightly deserved, she wanted to find out as much about Ravenwilde as she could. Therefore, she asked in a tone of mild interest, "How long has he been out of the country?"

"Oh, these eight or ten years, at least," Judith answered, somewhat calmer. "You were not yet out, and I dare say never heard any of the scandalous stories circulated about him in the city."

"Who is his stepmama? I don't remember hearing about a Duchess of Ravenwilde, and I'm certain I haven't met the lady."

"No, you wouldn't know her. Soon after her husband's death, she moved away to Ireland, where she had relatives, and after a suitable period of mourning, she married Lord Blackthorn, who they say is very old, but as rich as a nabob, so it's no wonder she consented to be his wife. Really, what other choice did she have? Most of her first husband's property and funds were entailed and she was left with a mere competence. What with Ravenwilde being as clutch-fisted as a miser, the poor woman was left with not much choice but to marry again, and that as soon as the proprieties would permit."

"Well, I'm sure I don't know what else she could have done, nor do I care very much," Sarah replied, affecting a boredom she was far from feeling. "I collect the lady was much younger than Ravenwilde's father?"

"Yes, quite a lot younger; very near the present duke's age, as a matter of fact. Unfortunately, there was no issue from the marriage, or I'm persuaded the old duke would have left her much better situated than he did when he died."

"Well, at any rate," Sarah answered easily, "all that happened a long time ago, and I don't imagine many people will continue to hold Ravenwilde's youthful follies against him, especially not the mamas with marriageable daughters to fire off. It has been an observation of mine these many years that money and a title make up for a multitude of sins. But it's nothing to us. I doubt I shall ever see the gentleman again, so there's nothing to upset yourself over."

"Randolph tells me that he was paying particular attention to you and went so far as to inquire if you were attending the ball on Friday," Judith persisted suspiciously.

"Yes, but I am sure Randolph told you what my answer was and I am equally sure the gentleman was merely being polite to the county spinster. You can't accuse *him* of being a fortune hunter. From what you say, he has quite a fortune of his own and has no need of mine. Now, let us forget it, Judith, for I must finish dressing for dinner. You know how Randolph hates for dinner to be delayed."

This warning had the desired effect of hastening Judith to her own room to prepare for dinner, and Sarah was left with even more thoughts to tease her already troubled mind.

Dinner that evening was not a comfortable affair. No sooner had the servants withdrawn after serving the first course than Lord Sandover began in his ponderous way to catechize Sarah about her encounter with Ravenwilde. Making a great effort to control her sorely tried temper, and succeeding admirably, Sarah again recounted an expurgated version of their chance meeting in the wood. "For you must know," she said for what seemed to her the dozenth time," "that I had taken Casper into the wood for a run and had intended picking some blueberries if I should happen upon any. I assure you, no one could have been more surprised than I when the gentleman presented himself through the bushes."

"Well, I must say you took a great deal upon yourself when you informed him that Judith and I would attend Friday's ball and that he would no doubt enjoy our company. In fact, nothing could be further from the truth," Lord Sandover informed her pompously.

Remembering Ravenwilde's twinkling eyes and ready laughter, Sarah could not resist saying with a twinkle of her own, "No, you are perfectly right. Ravenwilde would not enjoy your company at all."

"Sarah," Judith asked in darkening tones, "are you being impertinent?"

Flashing her sister a surprised, innocent glance, Sarah answered, "Why, no, sister. It is only that it is obvious to the meanest intellect that Ravenwilde has absolutely nothing in common with you and Randolph except possibly a property line."

"Well, I should hope not," Lady Sandover answered somewhat smugly. "One is forced to acknowledge that his birth is unexceptionable, but he has comported himself in such a way these many years as to put himself beyond the pale of polite society, don't you agree, Randolph?"

"Yes, my dear, but since he is who he is, the title, you know, one is forced to accept him. We cannot give him the cut direct, but one is not obliged to make of him a boon companion. I was gratified to learn from him that he will be posting to London in a few week's time. He is here only for a short time in order that he might set to rights a few minor problems which have arisen concerning his estates. And to give the devil his due, one must admit that his lands have been managed excellently. Our bailiff has engaged his bailiff in conversation in the village on different occasions, and he says that Ravenwilde, even in his absence, has kept in close contact with him through correspondence and has at all times taken an admirable interest in his lands and tenants."

Sarah was listening to these comments with far more interest than her carefully cultivated air of indifference would indicate. So the gentleman was going to London, was he? She wondered what would be the chances of her meeting him there and decided they would be very good indeed. In spite of what her sister said about the duke's being beyond the pale of polite society, she was more inclined to agree with what her brother-in-law said. Few, if any, would chance denying Ravenwilde access to their homes and social events. His remarks also had reinforced her own beliefs, as she had commented to her sister earlier, that his title and fortune must always make him welcome even to the highest stickler. And besides, no one knew in what manner he had spent his time while out of the country, and so far as his earlier indiscretions were concerned, no one knew better than Sarah that the ton soon lost interest in an old scandal when a new one (and surely there had been many in the past ten years!) presented itself.

Of course, his reappearance on the London scene would cause comment and speculation for a short time, but all things considered, Sarah was quite sure he would be welcomed with open arms. While there might be many gentlemen who would be considered eligible, there were few, if any, who could lay claim to being *as* eligible as Ravenwilde. In addition to his aforementioned title and fortune, the gentleman was pleasing to behold, and while his manners might be a trifle more easy than some would desire, certainly there was nothing about him that would disgust. Yes, she thought wryly, his grace would be most welcome during the coming season.

Sarah and Lady Sandover retired to the small drawing room and left Lord Sandover to drink his brandy in solitary splendor, but Sarah's sigh of relief as they left the table was premature, for they had barely settled themselves comfortably when Judith began a monologue that to Sarah's astonishment seemed to indicate that she had either forgotten or never heard when Sarah assured her repeatedly that she was indeed leaving for London, alone, within the week.

"I don't think we shall travel to London for the season this year, Sarah," Lady Sandover began in her droning voice. "Randolph and I are agreed that the three of us will be much more comfortable here at home, and since you have attracted quite enough suitors here from which to choose, we see no reason to subject ourselves to the upheaval of our lives that must attend a removal to London. My own health is such at this time that dear Randolph thinks the rigors of a London season will be too much for my constitution to bear and has already informed the servants in Grosvenor Square that we will not be opening the house this year. Of course, it is not merely our own comfort we are considering, but that of dear little Charles as well. It must always be difficult for a child to be removed from his permanent home, and since he will be going away to Eton next year, we much prefer to remain here with him, where we might enjoy more of his company for as long as we have him with us. It is a melancholy truth that once a child leaves home for school, some part of him is lost forever to his parents."

Sarah privately thought that it was a shame that a *great* part, if not all, of the little monster could not be lost, for it would be a good thing, but she naturally kept these observations from his doting parent. Instead, she answered, "You must be aware, Judith, that I am even now making plans and preparations for my own removal within the week. It is indeed kind of you to include me in your family plans, but I have told you repeatedly, I mean to set myself up independently."

Smiling on her as one might smile on a demented child, Judith sighed and said with a reasonableness that quite set Sarah's teeth on edge, "But I simply cannot allow that. I thought I had made myself quite clear on that point."

Responding in kind and with a smile quite as insincere as her sister's, Sarah said, "It seems we have been talking at cross purposes these past days, for *I* was equally sure that I had made it quite clear to

31

you that I am determined to go. I have already instructed my servants in Brook Street to hold the house in readiness for my arrival and have been corresponding with Aunt Silvia these past few weeks concerning her living with me as chaperon. Not that I really need a chaperon at my age, but I knew it would satisfy not only your sense of the proprieties, but those of our friends and acquaintances as well for me to have a respectable older female in attendance, and no one can deny the respectability of Aunt Silvia."

"Not her respectability nor her permissiveness," Judith answered with some asperity. "Everyone knows you are able to wrap her around your little finger. It was always thus, even when we were children. The silly woman positively dotes on you, and you needn't try to convince me that she would be able to exercise the least restraint upon you."

"Very well, then, I won't," Sarah answered with equanimity, but since her sister had grown progressively redder of face and seemed to Sarah to be in imminent danger of going off in an apoplectic fit, she said in soothing tones, "You really must calm yourself, Judith. You are making far too much over what is really a small matter. I fear for your health if you continue to allow yourself to become agitated to such a degree."

"If you had the least bit of feeling for my health, you would not persist in this bird-witted scheme of yours to set up your own establishment. I am sure Father had no such thing in mind when he willed you those two properties," Judith answered petulantly, but somewhat more calmly.

"And pray, what do you suppose he *did* have in mind? It is my belief that he intended all along that I should be independent. There is no other reasonable explanation for his extraordinary actions," Sarah pointed out.

"You obviously will not listen to me, but I must tell you that Randolph will have something to say in the matter, and I am persuaded that even you must recognize his superior wisdom and be guided by him."

"Then you have persuaded yourself of a great misconception," Sarah retorted. "I would beg of you not to encourage Randolph to try to dissuade me, and I would remind you yet again that he in no way stands as my guardian. I am of age, yes, and past that mark, as you have been at pains to point out to me on numerous occasions, and I can and shall do as I please. I would further advise you that no one will take more than a passing interest in my doings unless you and Randolph make a great fuss over it. If it is seen by everyone that our parting has been an amicable one, little if any comment will arise. However, I warn you, Judith, how the ton receives this is up to you. If you choose to make an unnecessary issue of it, the results will be on your head, for I mean to go and there's an end to it."

Thus saying, Miss Windemere left the room with all the dignity she could muster, sought out her maid, and instructed her to hasten with the packing, for she was desirous of leaving for London at the earliest possible moment.

Pacing to and fro in her room, Sarah thought she was possibly more angry than she had ever been in her life. Judith and Randolph had tried her patience over and over in the past year since her father's death, but this latest contretemps was the outside of enough! It was not enough that they had thrown her at the head of every eligible gentleman they could round up and nagged her incessantly to choose

33

from among them a husband, but they had attempted (with a great deal of success here in the country) to hedge her in on all sides and restrict her every movement. They were continually reminding her of what was expected of a lady of quality (as if she didn't know) and criticizing her every move. They were mortified if they found her in open and frank conversation with a gentleman and positively scandalized should she be so daring as to laugh out loud in the presence of a member of the opposite sex. A lady must always be of a shy and retiring nature, and she must never, never let a gentleman even suspect that she possessed any *intelligence* at all. And to make matters worse (in her sister's opinion), she was disgustingly healthy, and everyone knew that a gentleman preferred his lady to be interestingly weak. Why, Sarah had never felt even the slightest inclination to faint, and she could sit in the saddle almost as long as any gentleman in the county and still be ready to dance half the night away. Not that she had actually *danced* these past twelve months of mourning, but she had certainly been known to enjoy her share of dancing before her father's death.

All this Sarah had borne with outward placidity, having no desire to come to cuffs with her family. But this latest was not to be borne!

Was it possible? Could Judith actually imagine that if she simply ignored or refused to take seriously Sarah's intention of removing herself from Lord Sandover's home, Sarah would simply abandon the scheme? Ah, yes she did! Sarah had heard her many times giving as her opinion that a naughty child should be ignored and he would soon see that his unacceptable behavior was not bothering anyone and abandon it. And now Judith had the gall to reduce her to the position of a naughty child whose behavior was unacceptable and, therefore, to be ignored. No, it was definitely not to be borne!

Sarah knew she was in a dangerous mood. It was a very good thing, and even in her seething anger she recognized the truth of it, that no opportunity arose for her to rebel overtly, for she was in just such a mood that she might kick over the traces and damn the consequences.

Fortunately the week passed without incident, and on the night before her departure, Sarah was able to speak calmly to her sister. "I shall bid you farewell now, Judith, for I mean to get an early start tomorrow and I doubt you will be about when I leave. I pray you will not worry yourself unnecessarily about me, for you know I will have Aunt Silvia with me, and however little you might think of her ability to exert influence over me, you must know that she would never countenance anything that might invite remark. Besides Aunt Silvia, I shall also have all the servants, who have known us from the nursery, and you know well how conscious they are of what is due a member of the house of Windemere and how jealously they guard our reputation."

Far from being reassured by these utterances, Judith's countenance grew colder. "You don't deceive me for a moment with all your honeyed words, Sarah. We both of us are well aware that the servants in Brook Street are as blind to your faults as is our aunt. You were always a great favorite of theirs, and not one of them would venture to say you nay no matter what wheedle you might choose to cut."

"Very well, sister, if you refuse to be comforted, I will bid you goodnight. Should I not see Randolph before I leave, please convey to him my thanks for his hospitality," Sarah answered as she rose to leave the room.

After an excited Casper finally settled down comfortably at his mistress's feet, the journey into London passed uneventfully, with Sarah gazing through the window of the carriage at the familiar landscape while her maid, Alice, dozed in the far corner and occasionally, to the gentle amusement of her mistress, emitted a most unladylike snore.

After passing the first few miles in profound relief at finally being actually on her way, not just to London, but to independence, Sarah began thinking on the things she must do upon her arrival. The house, she knew, would require none of her attention. The servants were all old retainers from her father's day, and for the first time Sarah realized that her father had shuffled the servants around from the various estates until he had managed to fill the London house and Foxborough with all her favorites. Dear, dear, father, she thought now, barely able to check the tears that threatened to escape. He must have known how desperately I would need their support.

No, the household would require nothing more than her presence, but it had been over a year now since she had ventured into any society other than a few small country dinner parties with family and close friends. But now the period of formal mourning for her father was passed and she knew her wardrobe to be in a sad state. Styles changed from season to season, and for the past year her purchases had been limited to ribbons to refurbish a favorite bonnet and the small necessities such as gloves, stockings, and unmentionables. While the traveling gown she now wore was undoubtedly becoming and of the very best materials, the discerning eye would know at a glance that it was not of the latest mode. While Miss Windemere was not particularily concerned about the opinion of others, it was a source of personal satisfaction for her to know herself to be well dressed. She was second to none when it came to taste and that particular sense of what was right and becoming. Even Judith grudgingly admitted Sarah's superiority in the realm of cut and color and fashion and always bowed to her judgment.

Sarah herself was no real beauty. She was too tall to be fashionable, her hair was a rich brown with auburn highlights, her eyes neither blue nor brown, but gray, which was a color never in style, and her mouth much too generous in size. In short, she did not possess the petite figure, the blond curls, blue eyes and bow-shaped mouth that had been the rage now for several years. However, she knew just how to dress her tall form and exactly how to arrange her brown tresses. Her generous mouth was seen most often in an engaging smile which showed perfect white teeth, and her gray eyes were usually twinkling with good humor. All this, plus a sunny disposition, led some to believe that Miss Windemere was in fact a very beautiful lady. She was also possessed of an abundance of charm and good manners which made her a favorite with servants and the highest sticklers of the ton alike.

Yes, her first priority must be to refurbish her own wardrobe, but she was equally determined that Aunt Silvia be persuaded to let her do the same for her. Sarah had no need to practice economy, but Aunt Silvia, while not poor by any means, lived on a limited income from her late husband and was obliged to forgo the more extravagant pleasures of town life.

Silvia Mashburne was a small, lively lady of some fifty years. In her youth she had possessed both a sweet beauty and a disposition which attracted the attentions of several eligible gentlemen and quite a few ineligible ones. When it came to choosing a husband, she settled on Mr. Jonas Mashburne, a suitor who ranked somewhere between the eligible and ineligible. Never a slow top, she knew exactly what she was doing when she married Jonas. She knew that she would always be accepted by the ton because of who she was, but that she and Jonas would never have the money necessary to maintain the standard of living to which she had been born. But she loved him with all her heart, and was fortunate that he adored her until the day he died. Her only regret was that the marriage was not blessed with children, but after Sarah's birth, even this regret diminished somewhat. She absolutely doted on the child, and Sarah grew up basking in the warmth of an uncritical devotion. Her own dear Aunt Silvia became her favorite person in all the world (with the exception of her father), and when she decided to set up her own establishment, she did not even consider any other companion. And indeed there could be no better companion found anywhere. Mrs. Mashburne's qualifications as companion to Sarah were impeccable. She was a lady with breeding and background, her taste and manners were unexceptionable, she was up to snuff on every suit, knowing all the pitfalls of society and just how to avoid them, and best of all, she and Sarah would rub along together very well, enjoying as they did a mutual respect and affection.

Lost in such musings as these, Sarah found that the trip progressed smoothly, and much sooner than she had expected, the carriage came to a halt outside a smallish but very attractive house from which light was cascading from an open door. Picking up Casper, who had spent the better part of the trip sleeping at her feet, Sarah alighted from the coach with the help of a footman who had hurried down the short flight of steps leading to the open door.

"Why, Jack," Miss Windemere exclaimed, "I thought to find you in the stables. How fine you look in your footman's uniform!"

Grinning widely, Jack answered, "Welcome home, Miss Sarah. Stevens needed another footman in the house and kindly brought me in from the stables. I miss the horses, but we only keep a few now, as you know, and we don't need so many stable hands."

"Are you happy in the house?" Sarah asked.

"Oh, yes, ma'am," he assured her. "It took a little getting used to, but we're all happy as grigs here now."

After a few more minutes conversing with Jack, Sarah was assured that he was quite satisfied in his new post. Handing over the tired and still-sleepy Casper into his care, she asked him to take the pup to the kitchens and see that he was fed and then taken outside for a bit of exercise. "Then if you will, have him put in my rooms. I intend that he be a house dog while we are here."

The butler, Stevens, who had been with her family as long as Sarah could remember, was waiting patiently at the door. "Ah, Stevens, how nice to see you again. Are you well?"

"Fine, Miss Sarah. May I say how glad we all are, and I'm speaking for the entire staff, to have you with us again?"

"Thank you, Stevens. I'm very glad to be here. Has my aunt arrived yet?"

"Yes, Miss Sarah. I think you'll find her in the Yellow Saloon. Shall I order tea?"

"That would be lovely. I'll just go and wash off some of the travel dirt. Order tea for about fifteen minutes and please inform my aunt that I'll be with her directly," Sarah instructed as she walked toward the winding staircase. Stopping on the first landing, she looked back at Stevens, who was watching her fondly from below, and said, "Oh, Stevens, it is *so* good to be here with you again."

"Yes, Miss Sarah," he agreed, smiling, his blue eyes twinkling with something very close to mischief, "it will be almost like old times."

"Yes, old friend," Sarah replied almost wistfully, "just like old times."

Chapter 3

A very short time later, Sarah joined her aunt in the Yellow Saloon and the two ladies had a lovely time exclaiming how glad they were to be together again. Mrs. Mashburne enjoyed shedding a few tears over her dear Sarah and fussing over her comfort. "For you must be tired, my love, after so long a journey."

"Nonsense, my dear Aunt," Sarah answered with a decided twinkle in her eyes. "I am not yet so advanced in years as to be knocked up by a mere day's journey."

Smiling fondly at her irreverent niece, Mrs. Mashburne said, "Silly child, of course you are not, but the roads are not of the best, and no matter how well sprung your carriage may be, and I'm sure it is as good as can be, even a day's journey can weary one.

But I can see you are in glowing health, so I shan't fuss any more. I remember how you hated above all things to be fussed over, even as a child."

Impulsively holding out her hand to her aunt, Sarah said, "Dear Aunt, how well I remember the care you took of me after my mother died. How can I ever repay you for your unselfish devotion?"

"Now you are being foolish beyond permission, my dear," her aunt answered somewhat mistily. "Any care I gave to you brought me quite as much pleasure as it did you, so we'll speak no more about that. But I must and will tell you how grateful I am that you have invited me to stay with you for the season. The prospect of another season with you has quite given me a new lease on life. I can admit to you now that I have been bored to distraction this past year."

"You too?" Sarah asked, the twinkle returning to her fine gray eyes. "Can you imagine what it was like living with Judith and Randolph for a full year? I can tell you, Aunt Silvia, it was a blessing the day those two met and made a match of it, for it would have been an absolute crime had either of them been leg-shackled to anyone else. I shouldn't wish that fate on my worst enemy."

"Quite so, my dear," Mrs. Mashburne agreed, entering easily into Sarah's mood. "One can almost believe it was divine intervention, for you must know that Lady Coxcrow was pushing very hard for a match between Randolph and her youngest daughter."

"Not little Lettie!" Sarah exclaimed. "Why, he would have destroyed that gentle creature within six months."

"Yes," agreed Mrs. Mashburne. "It was indeed fortunate that Judith decided to marry him, for when

Judith really sets her mind on something, there is no stopping her."

"Well, she has been stopped now," Sarah answered grimly. "You know she was adamantly opposed to my setting up my own establishment."

"I knew she would be," her aunt answered, "and while I don't know all the particulars as to why you decided upon such a move, I am very glad you did not allow her to dissuade you. Please believe me when I assure you that I would feel the same had you not chosen *me* for a companion."

"Dearest Aunt, whom else would I choose?"

"Well, as to that, I am quite sure there are any number of ladies who would be glad to be in my shoes at this moment. However, I feared Judith would choose someone for you, and her choice certainly would not have been me."

"Perhaps she would have *tried* had she been persuaded that I was serious in my resolve. But, you see, she didn't really believe me until the very last minute, even though I assured her any number of times of my intentions. She seemed to take the position that if she ignored my plans, I would abandon them. I think the silly creature actually thinks I planned the whole thing just to annoy her."

"I shouldn't be at all surprised, my love, for she is a remarkably self-centered creature."

"Yes, but let us forget Judith and Randolph and leave all unpleasantness behind us. We are going to have such a good time, you and I. First we must see to our wardrobes. I do not know about yours, but mine is deplorable. I haven't bought any new gowns in over a year. Tomorrow we shall go and enjoy a veritable spending orgy," Sarah enthused.

"My dear, you must know that I haven't the means for such extravagance, but I shall be delighted to accompany you. While my gowns are not *quite* new, yet I believe you will have no cause to be ashamed of me," Mrs. Mashburne answered, smiling.

"Silly love," Sarah chided gently, "you know I would not be ashamed of you in any event, but surely you will not deny me the pleasure of making you a present of one or two gowns? You know I pride myself on having the best eye in all of London for style," she continued in a cajoling fashion, "and I have so looked forward to making the two of us into the most dashing ladies the ton has seen in many a year. Although you are a widowed lady and I a spinster, neither of us is ready to stick our spoons into the wall as yet, and I fancy we can still turn a head or two."

"Stick our spoons into the wall?" Mrs. Mashburne asked in mock surprise. "Really, Sarah, where did you pick up such cant expressions?"

"Actually, dear Aunt," Sarah answered mischievously, "I *think* that particular phrase was learned from you."

"Naughty puss."

But finally the older lady consented to accepting a gift of one or two gowns from her beloved niece if it would make her happy, and the two ladies went upstairs arm in arm and in perfect harmony to prepare for bed.

The ladies set out the next day directly after breakfast and spent a tiring but most satisfactory morning at Sarah's favorite modiste, where they critically examined lengths of muslin, satin, and silk. Sarah gave it as her opinion that a gray satin had just enough blue in it to make Mrs. Mashburne's blue eyes positively irresistible to anyone who chanced to look into them and that a certain style was definitely *not* cut too low to be becoming for a lady of

Mrs. Mashburne's years. "For you must know, Aunt Silvia," Sarah added as a clincher, "that you are still a very attractive woman. Many are the young ladies just out of the schoolroom who would give half they possess to have your figure, and your face is as smooth as mine. You must tell me how you have contrived to stay so young."

"You are talking nonsense again, my love," the older lady replied, a lovely blush coloring her clear complexion a becoming pink. "It is you who should have the gray, for I declare it is exactly the color of your eyes."

Later as they were emerging from a small but very expensive shop where each lady had been persuaded to purchase half a dozen ravishing bonnets to match the gowns they had chosen earlier, they chanced to meet an old friend of Sarah's, Lady Ainsberry, who invited them to tea later in the afternoon. "We have so many things to discuss, dear Sarah. I have missed you dreadfully. You must tell me everything you have been doing these past months. I know you have been in mourning for your dear father, but wherever you are and no matter what circumstances, there is something of interest happening. You were always so full of life and benign mischief."

"Well, there you are wrong, Margaret. These past months have been unspeakably dull, but I shall be glad to hear about your doings."

When the ladies had parted company and Mrs. Mashburne and Sarah had proceeded on to the various shops to purchase half boots, evening slippers, day slippers, gloves, ribbons, stockings, reticules, and a lovely paisley shawl which Sarah declared to be just perfect for Mrs. Mashburne, they instructed John Coachman to drop them at Lady Ainsberry's home in Grosvenor Square, deliver the packages to Brook Street, and return for them in an hour.

"Now tell me, Margaret," Sarah encouraged her friend when they were settled with their tea, "what has been happening in town while I have been away? You must tell me all the *on dits.*"

"Actually not much has happened. Lady Cloverfield finally found a husband for Caroline—you know her, don't you? She was the middle daughter, the one with spots. I suppose the only thing that has happened worth mentioning is that the Duke of Ravenwilde is back in England. No one has seen him in London yet, but it is rumored that he will be in town for the season. I myself do not remember him. I think he fled the country the year before you and I made our come-outs."

Fortunately Sarah was bent over the tea tray replenishing her aunt's cup, and neither lady could see her face when Margaret so casually mentioned Ravenwilde. When she looked up, her features were composed and she was able to inform her friend and aunt that she already knew the duke was in England and had, as a matter of fact, met him.

"Never say so!" Margaret exclaimed, her eyes dancing with mirth. "And you had the audacity to tell me nothing had happened to you! All the unmarried ladies in London, not to mention their mamas, are dying to meet him, this in spite of the cloud under which he departed our shores, and you, buried as you were in the country, have stolen a march on all of them. Oh, Sarah, this is beyond anything wonderful. But come now, tell us all about him."

"I fear I must disappoint you, dear friend. It was the most casual of encounters, I assure you. His lands march with those of my brother-in-law's, and he paid a call on Lord Sandover to discuss some trifling mat-

46

ter concerning their respective gamekeepers. I really cannot tell you much more than that."

Mrs. Mashburne, who knew her niece better than anyone in the world, was very much aware of the carefully casual tones in which Sarah related her innocent tale even if Lady Ainsberry was not. However, the older lady held her tongue and merely listened to the two younger women.

"Really, Sarah," Margaret chided good-naturedly, "I am disappointed in you. You had the perfect opportunity to advance yourself with the duke before he came to London to be eaten alive by all the matchmaking mamas and you failed to take advantage of it. But never mind, tell me all about him. Is he really as handsome as they say? Does he give the impression of being a rake and a wastrel? He is spoken of by those who knew him before the scandal in deliciously palpitating undertones. They are all quivering with anticipation. Even though it is generally agreed that he is a danger and a threat to all *pure* damsels, the ton cannot wait to welcome him into their midst. But tell me, Sarah, what were your impressions?"

Choosing her words carefully, Sarah answered with a smile, "I hate to disappoint you yet again, Margaret, but I found the gentleman to be quite unexceptionable. It is true that he is out of the ordinary handsome. He is tall and has dark hair and eyes. His complexion, too, is rather dark. He has an easy smile and a graceful bearing. As to whether or not he is a rake, I really could not say, since my experience with rakes is very limited, but I can tell you he is *not* a wastrel. Even my brother-in-law is impressed with the conditions of his lands and tenants. It seems that even though he has been away, Ravenwilde has retained an active interest in his estates and has regularily posted instructions as to their management."

"Is that all you can tell me? I had hoped for the pleasure of spreading firsthand information before the gentleman arrives in town," Margaret complained with a twinkle in her lovely eyes.

Sarah only laughed to her friend's complaint, for she knew her to be the last person in London to spread gossip. She was always a sweet, gentle creature, and no one, least of all Sarah, had been surprised when one of the richest gentleman in the realm asked for her hand.

"The only other thing I can tell you is that he will be in London within a fortnight. He imparted this information to Lord Sandover himself. He will be a neighbor of yours, by the way, for he is going to open the house here in Grosvenor Square."

"Oh, splendid!" Margaret exclaimed. "I was afraid he would merely take rooms and leave the house vacant. I am opening the season with a ball in three weeks' time, and if I send an invitation around to his house now, perhaps I will be before any other hostesses and can bag him for my party first."

The conversation moved on to other subjects, and soon Sarah and Mrs. Mashburne took their leave. Sarah was unusually quiet during the drive home, and when Mrs. Mashburne ventured to comment on this, Sarah answered, "Oh, do forgive me, dear Aunt, I was woolgathering again. Judith was forever scolding me for doing so."

"You know I would never scold you, love, but I was wondering if the day's shopping coupled with the journey yesterday has not quite worn you out," her aunt answered mendaciously.

Sarah laughed and answered, "You are determined to make of me an old woman. I am a little fatigued, but not *completely* fagged out. Are you not tired?"

"Yes, a little. If you don't mind, I think I shall lie down and rest for an hour before dinner," Mrs. Mashburne answered.

Actually, a quiet time spent in a comfortable coze with Sarah would have been sufficient to restore the older lady, but with the sixth sense she had always possessed where Sarah was concerned, she knew her niece needed and wanted some time to be alone and therefore took herself off to her room directly they arrived home.

Sarah opened the door to her own bedchamber to be greeted by an ecstatic Casper, who could still not quite believe the freedom and luxury he was currently enjoying. Everyone in the house was kind to him—this in spite of the small problems his playful antics often caused the staff—but while he was friendly with everyone, his devotion was reserved for his beloved mistress, from whom, as he sensed in the way of dogs, sprang all his good fortune. Taking the pup onto her lap and gently stroking his soft coat, Sarah let her mind wander to her recent conversation with Margaret.

She was aware that while she had not actually been thinking about the Duke of Ravenwilde, the memory of her encounter with him had been lurking just barely below the surface of her consciousness, and it took only the mention of his name to bring total recall of every word that had passed between them, and every feature of his face and form.

She knew she could have described to Margaret and Aunt Silvia in minute detail how his lips parted in ready laughter, how the laughter really started in his soft brown eyes, and how the tone of his voice conveyed laughter even when he was not actually laughing with his eyes and mouth. She could have described his teasing voice, the deep creases that ran from nose to mouth, his strong chin, the crinkles around his eyes and the creases in his forehead (there were four of them). She could have told them he had long slender fingers and that he moved with a lithe grace that was totally unexpected in one of his size. And even alone in her room, she blushed to remember the familiarity with which they had conversed, almost as if they had known each other from the cradle. She supposed that such easy discourse came naturally to a gentleman of the duke's stamp, but for Sarah, always a pattern card of decorum in spite of her lively sense of humor, such behavior was completely foreign.

He must think me shockingly forward, she thought, and determined anew that should she meet him again, she would conduct herself with perfect propriety. Of course, he might not even remember her, a disturbing voice within reminded her. Ah, well...

While Sarah was wrestling with these unwelcome thoughts, his grace, the Duke of Ravenwilde was sitting at a huge desk in the library of his country estate tidying up such minor details concerning the estate as required his attention. Another week and he would be off to London. In the past years, the duke had faced many and varied dangers. His life and safety had been in jeopardy any number of times—indeed, almost the whole of the time he had been away from England had been lived in various degrees of danger—but he had never faced a situation he dreaded more than the coming season.

However, a letter from his grandmother, which had arrived some two weeks previously, reminded him that he must indeed begin a life in keeping with his birth and responsibilities. The old lady had reminded him of his duties as head of the family, namely that he must marry and produce an heir. "For you are well aware," she had written, "that if you should die without a son, your distant cousin, a hardened gambler and determined wastrel, would inherit your title and estates. We owe it to your ancestors, your father and his father, and even those before them, not to let the title be disgraced or the wealth squandered away by such as he. Even though I am not a Ravenwilde, but your maternal grandmother, still I feel the responsibility. Come to London, my son, and seek a wife. Surely, among all the beauties on the marriage mart, you will find one who will please you."

Ravenwilde had never felt the least desire to marry anyone. True, these past few years he had had no opportunity to meet eligible ladies, but even before he left England, he had never given marriage a thought except to devise ways of avoiding it. It was not that he did not like women. In his younger days it could be said that he liked them only too well, but he had never met one with whom he felt the slightest inclination to spend the rest of his life.

His charm and good looks, not to mention the wealth and title to which everyone knew he would one day ascend, had made him a prime target for matchmaking mamas ever since he came down from Oxford. However, by being extremely careful in his dealings with young ladies, he had managed very successfully to avoid matrimony without actually offending anyone. He had left no broken hearts behind, for he was always careful to break off any flirtation that threatened to become serious long before the young lady's affections were seriously engaged. His only trophies were a few bruised egos, and none of them was very badly damaged. He had taken his pleasures among the demimonde and the experienced widows of the ton or the young matrons with compliant husbands. While he was abroad, there was scarcely time or opportunity for more than the briefest encounters, and he found that this suited him very well.

Ravenwilde was well aware of the scandalous gossip which had been circulated when he left England and would not have lifted a finger to squelch it even if he could. Nor would he now defend his honor or reputation. No, not with a single word! Let the world think what it would. He knew his grandmother would say that he was asking a great deal of a young lady to expect her to have faith in his honor without knowing all the facts, but if he was going to marry, and he knew that he must, he hoped to find just such a lady.

She need not love him, but she must respect him. Until his return, his grandmother had not even been in possession of the facts, but she had never lost faith in him. He thought that she alone in all of England (outside certain members of the government) believed him to be honorable. After he had sworn her to secrecy, he had put her in possession of all the facts concerning his years abroad and had almost been unmanned when he saw the tears streaming down her lined cheeks and the beatific smile on her lips. "And your father knew what you were doing before he died?" she had asked, and when he replied in the affirmative, the garrulous old woman had said simply, "Thank God."

Thus far, the only young lady he had met since coming home was Miss Windemere, but the circumstances of their meeting, for some reason, seemed to exclude her from any list of eligible ladies. Perhaps it was her declaration that she would not marry without love, an emotion for which the duke had very little use, and a trap into which he had no intention of falling. And yet she was charming, and a little beauty. No, not little, and not really a beauty, and yet there was a certain something about her which seemed to transcend beauty.

No, she would not make a suitable wife, but she would be a very comfortable friend. Perhaps when he went up to London she could fill him in on some of the eligible ladies of the ton. He would have no hesitation in asking her; he felt he could discuss almost anything with her. Yes, he was looking forward to furthering their friendship.

Having settled his affairs as far as he was able, the Duke of Ravenwilde set forth for London a week later and was soon well established in Grosvenor Square, a place for which he felt a particular fondness, for he had spent many happy days there before his father remarried. He found himself enjoying town life to a degree he had not believed possible. He visited his tailor and renewed his membership at his favorite clubs. He met a number of old acquaintances, and for the most part they were glad to have him back among their numbers. But the big hurdle was yet to be faced. He found a prodigious number of invitations awaiting him and immediately accepted the one from Lady Ainsberry. He was not acquainted with the lady, but Lord Ainsberry had been a particular friend of his youth and he was anxious to renew the friendship.

He presented himself promptly at nine o'clock on the following Friday evening at Lady Ainsberry's ball, and after bowing over the hand of his hostess, he found himself pumping the hand of his old friend Lord Ainsberry. "Ravenwilde, it's good to see you, old man. Let's have lunch at the club tomorrow and talk over old times, eh?"

"I didn't know you were acquainted with his grace," Lady Ainsberry said to her husband with a speaking look.

"Acquainted with Ravenwilde? Of course I am, my dear. We were at Harrow and Oxford together and were good friends for many years."

Margaret turned to the duke and saw the laughter lurking in his brown eyes. An answering smile touched her lips as she said, "Your grace, you must come to dinner one night soon. I have heard whispers concerning my husband's decadent youth, no one is willing to enlighten me fully. Perhaps you will be kind enough to do so."

"Believe me, ma'am," the duke answered solemnly, "your husband was the soul of propriety."

"Coming it a little too brown, your grace," the lady answered before turning to greet yet another guest and the duke wandered off into the ballroom.

As had been predicted in many quarters, the Duke of Ravenwilde was accepted back into the ton with open arms. Within the hour, he had been simpered over by no less than twenty fond mamas and introduced to their aspiring offsprings. However bored he might be, he never let it be seen, and he handled each matron with tact and charm.

When he had a moment to himself, he began to scan the room in an effort to find someone with whom he might converse with some degree of intelligence. Thus far he had managed to abstain from dancing, but he knew that unless he attached himself to someone very soon, he would be pressed into leading some blushing debutante onto the floor.

When his gaze fell upon Sarah, he had the distinct impression that she had been watching him, but she turned away before meeting his eye. Nevertheless, he made his way through the crowded room to her side.

"Miss Windemere," he said.

Affecting a graceful curtsy, Sarah murmured, "Your grace."

Holding her hand for perhaps a fraction longer than necessary, the duke said with a decided twinkle in his eyes, "My, aren't we proper tonight? The last time we met you were not so formal."

"For which I apologize, sir. You must think me shockingly rag-mannered."

"I think you charming," he answered.

Ignoring his remark, Sarah asked, "Are you enjoying town life?"

"Actually, I am enjoying it. I did not expect to, but there you are. Life is full of little surprises, isn't it? For instance, I was surprised to see you turn your head to avoid looking at me, and I imagine you were surprised that I would, after so obvious a cut, seek you out," he answered playfully.

Blushing furiously, Sarah stammered, "Your grace, really,...that is, I had no intention of cutting you. Oh, you're roasting me," she said, seeing the twinkle in his eyes. "A gentleman would never use a lady thusly."

"No, probably not, but then we have already established that I am quite without manners, have we not?"

"Indeed we have not," she retorted, "for I have observed this evening that you can behave very prettily when you so choose. All the mamas are in alt over you."

"Ah, then, my pretty, you *were* watching me."

"I was doing no such thing," she denied, but realizing the absurdity of their conversation, could not prevent a gurgle of laughter from escaping her throat. "Wretched man. What will people think?"

"Very probably they will think we waltz beautifully together. Come, the music is starting now."

Before she could protest that she had promised this dance to someone else, she found herself on the floor being whirled expertly around and around. She was very much aware of his strong arms around her and the nearness of his broad chest. However, she controlled her fluttering heart and trembling hands and laughed into his brown eyes. "Now I am really in the suds. I had promised this dance, you know."

"Yes, I thought you had, and I also suppose your card is full for the rest of the evening. However, I was determined to have my waltz, and I intend to escort you to supper, also. I hope you have not been so unwise as to have promised that honor to another."

Actually, she had not, admitting to herself now that she had hoped Ravenwilde would ask her. "No, I haven't, and I would be honored to have your escort."

Smiling down at her in such a way as to cause her silly heart to do flipflops, he teased, "Now who is roasting whom?"

"Certainly not I, your grace," she answered demurely.

When the music ended, Ravenwilde took her arm and turned to escort her off the dance floor. Looking toward the door, he exclaimed, "What luck! There's my grandmother. Come, let me introduce you to her. She is a great favorite of mine, and I think you will soon see why."

Chapter 4

They made their way to the side of a small, elegantly dressed old lady whose face was wrinkled, but whose brilliant blue eyes and white hair still sparkled with life. Seeing them approach, the lady's lips parted in an uncommonly sweet smile, and she held out one gloved hand to Ravenwilde. "Well, my son, I see you took my advice and came to London. I am glad to see you."

Bowing over the small hand he held firmly but gently in his own, Ravenwilde said, "Ah, Grandmother, how could I refuse a summons from you? I tremble to think on the consequences of disobeying you."

"Fustian," the old lady replied with a twinkle in her eyes. "You will never change, will you?"

"Do you really want me to, my only love?" he asked with an answering twinkle in his own eyes.

Watching them, Sarah was amazed at the gentleness in Ravenwilde's voice and the softness in his eyes when he looked at his grandmother. So charmed was she by the tall, harsh-featured gentleman and the small, fragile lady that she was only made aware that Ravenwilde was addressing her when she heard her own name.

"Grandmother, I want you to meet Miss Sarah Windemere. Miss Windemere, this is my grandmother, the dowager Duchess of Bloomington."

Sarah curtsied deeply, then surprised Ravenwilde by rising and taking both the old lady's hands in her own, bending low, and kissing her on each cheek. "Dearest, dear ma'am," she said. "I had no idea you were already in town or I would have been to call. You needn't tell me how you are, for I can see you are in great good health. May I come to call soon?"

"Of course, my child. You know I would be greatly cast down if you did not. I missed you last season. Town was a very dull place without you."

"I see you ladies already know each other," Ravenwilde said, smiling on them both.

"Indeed we do," Sarah answered, leading the old lady to a comfortable chair and seeing her settled in it. "Your grandmother, although I did not know she was your grandmother until this very moment, and I are old friends. I owe her more than I can possibly repay."

"Nonsense," the duchess replied. "It is I who owe you for giving me the pleasure of your young company."

"I never knew you craved young company, Grandmother. As I remember, you were used to refer to the debutantes as silly misses who all together didn't have enough sense to get in out of the rain."

"Well, and so they are," retorted the old woman, "but Sarah is a different breed, and I could see that from the start."

Laughing, Sarah replied, "You flatter me, ma'am. The truth is, your grace, that I was as silly a miss as ever left the schoolroom. The year of my come-out, my dear Aunt Silvia was laid low with a slight inflammation of the lungs, and since I had no mother to present me, my father made one of the few mistakes of his life by choosing a distant cousin of ours to chaperon me. Cousin Nell is a charming scatter-brain who assumed I knew far more than I did about how to comport myself in society. Consequently, I was on the verge of committing a dreadful solecism which must have had disastrous effects upon my reputation and placed me in a most unfavorable light with the ton. Your grandmother rescued me and was kind enough thereafter to keep an eye on me and help me avoid the thousand and one pitfalls a green girl fresh from the schoolroom might fall into during her first season. She was kindness itself, and I am convinced that I owe to her the fact that I am not today a complete social outcast."

"Perhaps I helped a little, my child, but your own good sense and breeding would have prevented any serious blunders. I just happened to be close by when you needed an older head. Now, we'll talk no more about it. Harry, please see if you can find me a glass of champagne."

The old lady watched fondly until Ravenwilde's broad back was lost from view in the press of the crowd, then turned to Sarah and asked, "How did you happen to meet my grandson?"

Sarah repeated to her an altered version of her

encounter with Ravenwilde in the woods and ended by saying, "And I haven't seen him again until tonight. So you see, we are not really well acquainted."

"That is a circumstance I hope to see corrected," the duchess answered softly. "Harry is a good man, my dear. Do not let the town wags convince you otherwise."

"You love him very much, don't you, ma'am?" Sarah asked softly.

"He is all I have left in the world," the old lady answered sadly. "My one desire is to see him happily married; then I can die peacefully."

In an effort to cheer the old lady and put their conversation on a lighter note, Sarah answered, "The way the mamas and their daughters have been fawning over him this night, I am sure your wish will come true before the season is out. But as for dying in peace, ma'am, you know you will have to stay around long enough to peek into his nursery and satisfy yourself that all is well there."

"Well, perhaps," the old lady admitted with a twinkle, "but still, my fondest wish is to see him happily settled. And you, my dear, have you not yet met anyone for whom you can feel the slightest tendre?" Seeing Sarah color rosily, she added, "Now don't go missish on me, Sarah. You know I only ask because I am concerned for your welfare."

"I know, ma'am, and I am sorry to disappoint you. Perhaps you haven't heard that I have set up my own establishment with Aunt Silvia to chaperon me," Sarah answered.

"No, I hadn't heard, but I am glad. Tell me, Sarah, how did you manage to escape Judith and Sandover?"

Laughing at the lady's candor, Sarah replied, "You must know it was not easy. However, I finally convinced Judith that I was determined in my resolution to leave the nest and live my own life. I am afraid she is very angry with me, and I am ashamed to admit that I was provoked into losing my temper and saying some things that perhaps would have been better unsaid. However, it is all over now, and since she and Randolph plan to remain in the country this season, she and I both will have ample time to get over our harsh words."

The two continued to converse amicably, the old lady giving it as her opinion that it would take a saint to live with Judith without coming to cuffs with her and relating to Sarah some amusing incidents that had happened in her life since the two had last met. When Ravenwilde returned with the champagne, Sarah excused herself to seek out her aunt. After being reminded by Ravenwilde that she was to go in with him to supper, she left her two friends and made her way to Mrs. Mashburne, who had unobtrusively been watching Sarah's movements since she first began to converse with Ravenwilde. She allowed none of the disquiet she felt to show in the countenance she presented to Sarah, but there was a nagging worry in her mind. It could be disastrous if the child (for despite Sarah's age, Mrs. Mashburne still thought of her as a child) should form a lasting attachment for the duke. It would break Mrs. Mashburne's heart to see her beloved Sarah hurt, but at the moment she could think of no way to curb the interest she, who knew Sarah so well, knew was growing for the duke in that young lady's heretofore untouched bosom. Ah well, it was early days yet, and perhaps her concern was a bit premature. Still, it wouldn't hurt to keep her eyes open.

Later, as they were riding home in the carriage after the ball, Mrs. Mashburne's fears surfaced once again when Sarah casually introduced Ravenwilde's name into their conversation, merely mentioning that the gentleman appeared to have made quite a conquest among the ton on his first venture into society after so long an absence.

"Yes," replied the older lady with equal casualness. "I fear it must always be so with gentlemen of wealth and title. That is not to say I think he should be banned from society, for I saw nothing in his conduct that would support such an action. I am merely remarking that gentlemen, no matter how they may behave, are always welcome, whereas a lady must constantly be on guard against the smallest action which might cause comment. By the by, my dear, I did not know you were on such intimate terms with Lady Bloomington."

"Yes. My friendship with her dates back to the year of my come-out. Without her to guide me in your absence, I fear I should have made a sad muddle of my first season. You know that Cousin Nell is a perfect widgeon, though a lovable one, and was quite unfit to introduce a green girl into society. However, I only learned tonight that the duchess is Ravenwilde's grandmother. She never mentioned it to me before, which is a very strange thing, for she positively dotes on the man. Tell me, Aunt Silvia, was what he did really so very bad?"

Choosing her words carefully, Mrs. Mashburne answered, "I really can't say, my love. Of course, I remember some of the gossip, but as you know, I never was one to encourage talebearing and was therefore not privy to most of the talk that was going around. From what I *did* hear, I concluded that a great deal of the talk was started by his stepmother and remember thinking that much of it was probably born out of jealousy, for everyone knew that the old duke's properties were entailed and that young Harry was bound to inherit. Since Clair had not produced an offspring, she must be left with a mere competence. I am sorry I cannot tell you more, but I have never moved in the same circles as the more *active* wags in our society."

"Yes, I know, dear Aunt, and that is one of the things I love so about you. But can you tell me what he was like when he was young?"

Maintaining the casual air she was far from feeling, Mrs. Mashburne answered, "I remember him as a polite, handsome boy whose eyes were always filled with mischievous laughter. He was always welcome, of course, at any gathering, and while he was attentive and courteous to everyone, he managed to elude the matchmakers and remain single. He comported himself as he ought always, and even though the hopes of many mamas and their daughters were dashed, it could never be said of him that he took advantage of anyone or raised false hopes in the breasts of any young lady. I believe he often engaged in dangerous and foolish races—which he invariably won—and wagered quite outrageous sums on such things as which fly would climb a wall faster, or the turn of a single card, and such nonsense as that, but it was never said that he ever overspent his income, which in those days was not nearly so great as it is today, and after all, those were and are the activities of most young men on the town. No, actually, I remember his behavior to be a pattern card of propriety the first few years he was on the town. It was later, after his father remarried, that all the gossip began, and I cannot say how much of it was true and how much was exaggeration."

She wanted very much to warn Sarah against forming too close a relationship with a man who had the reputation of a rogue and a rakehell, for whether or not the old gossip was true, it was obvious now that he was a man of experience. It had not escaped her attention, and indeed the notice of several others, that among all the young ladies at the ball, he had singled out only Sarah for a dancing partner—and a waltz at that. If nothing came of it, and there was scant chance that anything would, Sarah could be said to have set her cap for him, or worse, and while it would not damage his reputation, which was already in shreds, it could do irreparable harm to hers. However, she held her peace, sensing that any interference on that score would alienate her niece and put herself in a position where she would be of no use to Sarah in the future should she be needed either as a confidant or as an older lady to help smooth over any contretemps that might result from a flirtation with his grace.

Sarah arose early the next morning in spite of keeping such late hours the night before, and choosing the prettiest of her riding habits—a fawn-colored garment with a matching hat, both of which were trimmed with brown velvet, and the whole set off by York tan gloves and tan half boots to match— she set out on her chestnut mare for an early ride in the park with her groom a respectful distance behind. The Duke of Ravenwilde, who arrived at the gate to the park at the precise moment Sarah rode up, thought she made an altogether charming and refreshing sight, and smiling his easy, affable greeting, told her so.

"I fear you flatter me this morning, your grace," Sarah answered easily in spite of the increased rhythm of her heartbeats. "Last night's late hours have taken their toll. Aunt Silvia will say I should have stayed abed, but old habits die hard, and I have always been used to early rising. To me, 'tis the best part of the day, and I do not like to miss it."

"Yet another disillusionment, Miss Windemere, for I had always thought ladies loathe to bestir themselves until an advanced hour," the duke answered teasingly.

"And I, sir, was used to think gentlemen, following the example of Mr. Brummell, spent so much time on their toilette that they were never abroad before noon."

The duke laughed and replied, "I am afraid I will never be a regular man about town, Miss Windemere, but must always be considered a country bumpkin."

"Indeed yes," she answered with a twinkle in her eyes and a twitch at the corners of her mouth. "I wondered ought I mention the hay sticking from your ears and the mud on your boots."

They laughed together, and riding side by side, entered the park, which was almost deserted so early in the morning. The duke remarked that he had hoped an early ride would clear the cobwebs from his brain and enable him to solve a few minor problems that had been teasing him for several days, but when Sarah offered to ride on alone and leave him to think in peace, he assured her at once that he was very glad indeed for her company and that perhaps she could be of some help to him in his dilemma.

"But of course I shall help you if I can," she assured him at once. "You have only to tell me what it is you wish me to do."

Looking at her warmly he said, "Actually, there isn't a lot you can do except listen to my woes. You see, the thing of it is, I must take a wife, and the last thing in the world I want is to be leg-shackled. Marriage has never appealed to me, but my grandmother tells me, and I know it to be true, that I have a responsibility to produce an heir. My problem is that I have yet to meet a lady I wish to spend the rest of my life with. I know you will understand, since you have been pressured to take a husband against your will."

"Indeed I do," Sarah answered, trying to ignore the sinking feeling in the pit of her stomach. "But with you, it is a much more serious omission not to be married than it is with me. After all, I am not required to carry on the family name, whereas you, with your property and the title to consider, must have an heir. Tell me, your grace, what sort of female would be *least* objectionable to you? Perhaps there is one among my acquaintances to whom I could introduce you."

"Well, as to that," he answered seriously, "she must, of course, have breeding; I mean she must be a lady of quality. She need not have wealth, for I have more than I can ever spend, but I should like a degree of good looks—not necessarily a beauty, but one who carries herself well and is not ugly." The mischievous gleam entered his eyes again as he added, "I should hate to foist a host of ugly children onto the world."

"A host!" Sarah gasped. "Then we had best add a love of children to your list of qualifications."

"Good God, no!" the duke exclaimed. "For I was only joking. Truth to tell, I am not especially fond of children. One or two, if they be male children who can inherit, will be quite sufficient."

"And more than sufficient," Sarah answered, trying to suppress a gurgle of laughter, "if they are anything like the children of my acquaintance. I can see that children are *necessary,* and I suppose it is quite a different matter if they are one's *own* children, for it stands to reason that one *must* love one's own child, mustn't one? But thus far the reasons to fly into alt over mewling babies and gauche children who all too often take after the more unappealing of their two parents completely escapes me. Now what in the world are you laughing at, you abominable man?"

The duke, who had gone off into shouts of laughter, fought to regain his breath and answered, "I fear you would be considered a most unnatural female in most circles, my dear. I do hope you don't make a practice of spreading opinions such as those abroad."

"No, I don't," she answered sheepishly, "and I cannot imagine what it is about you that makes me display such a want of conduct. Really, sir, you somehow lead me into saying the most outrageous things! Even fortified with hartshorn and water, I fear my sister, Judith, would have a fit of the vapors if she could but hear me."

"That puts me in mind of another thing," the duke answered. "I cannot abide a female who is prone to vapors and spasms. Nor do I want a watering pot who is forever wrinkling my neckcloth with her tears."

"I see we have a formidable task ahead of us," Sarah answered, "for most ladies are reared to believe that an excess of sensibilities is what a gentleman admires."

"Perhaps some gentlemen do, although I am persuaded they are in the minority, but I do not," the duke answered emphatically, and sobering somewhat he added, "There is one other thing, Miss Windemere. I am sure you have heard rumors and gossip concerning my dishonorable past. The lady who becomes my wife must be willing and able to put those rumors aside and respect me as an honorable man. I have no intention of attempting to justify myself to anyone or to explain circumstances which I long ago judged to be best buried in the past. Do you think a lady who can respect someone with my reputation, without explanations, can be found?"

The duke was watching her intently while she attempted to formulate her answer. Finally, her clear gray eyes met his and she answered, "I have no doubt of it, your grace, for I am a female and I do not hesitate to assure you that while I have no problem picturing you as a mischievous, fun-loving, and perhaps at times thoughtless young man, it is beyond my imagination to see you as dishonorable. I feel quite sure you have never done a truly dishonorable thing in your life. Surely, when they learn to know you a little, other ladies will feel the same."

The duke felt a queer, unrecognizable jolt in the pit of his stomach, and looking away from her, he said wryly, "Perhaps you are right, but I haven't the confidence in the depths of human perception that you appear to have. Nonetheless, those are my requirements."

They rode on in silence for some few minutes, each lost in private thoughts. Finally Sarah broke the silence. "Perhaps you will be fortunate enough to make a love match, sir."

"I doubt it, my dear. I am not sure I believe in love, but in any event, one only has to look around at the married couples one knows to see that love matches are rare indeed."

"Yes, it does seem to be so," Sarah answered, "but you know, I was used to think, in my younger days, that falling in love must be the easiest thing in the world to do, and after observing some of the matches that were made, some of which portended to be love matches, I was quite sure of it, for surely no one in his right senses would put forth the least effort to either engage the affections of or have his own affections engaged by such as they, so it follows that it must be a thing one does without effort."

Perceiving that her companion had again gone off in a fit of whoops, Sarah asked, "Now what have I said that you should find so amusing?"

"Nothing at all, my dear," the duke answered when he was able and then asked, "Do you attend Lady Blackburne's ball on Friday next?"

They had by this time circled the park and arrived back at the gate where they would part. "Yes, I think so. Aunt Silvia is a particular friend of Lady Blackburne's and assures me that I, too, will like her very much. Are you acquainted with the lady?"

"Only slightly, and that in my youth. However, I remember her as a charming pea goose, but maturity may have changed her somewhat."

"Yes, I suppose it must. In my youth I was somewhat silly myself, as your dear grandmother can readily attest," Sarah replied.

"And now that you have reached an advanced age," the duke replied with an irrepressible chuckle, "you have settled down and are positively moldy. You must forgive me, Miss Windemere, for keeping you so long in the saddle. I keep forgetting that you are *quite* old and should be home with a *tense*."

"Wretch," she answered, "I am not quite *that* old, but you and I must admit to the fact that I cut my wisdom teeth years ago."

"Ah, yes, *many* years ago," the duke said with mock seriousness.

"Odious creature," she replied, dampened, "I see there is no conversing seriously with you, so I shall bid you good day."

He watched, smiling, as she turned her back to him and rode away. She really was a remarkable lady, he thought. Too bad she had her mind set on either a love match or remaining in the single state. What a waste! And what a luxury to be in a position to refuse marriage. He knew himself to be in no such a position. Already he was eight and thirty and no heir in sight. If there were a younger brother, a nephew, or even a responsible cousin to inherit, he would be content to live out his life without benefit of a wife, but there was no one, and rather than see the title and estates abused in the manner he knew his care-for-nobody cousin would do, he saw that it was clearly his duty to provide an heir, one who would care for the lands and tenants in the time-honored tradition of his family.

Sarah changed from her riding habit into a morning gown of pale-blue cambric, the elegant simplicity of which immediately bespoke a modiste of the first stare, and joined her aunt in the small, sunny dining parlor for breakfast. Mrs. Mashburne was dressed in pale yellow with the addition of a charming lace cap from which her still golden curls peaked in delightfully artless disarray.

When the ladies had greeted each other and filled their plates, Sarah said, "There is nothing like a morning ride to whet one's appetite," and proceeded to tell her aunt about meeting with Ravenwilde in the park. "That is not to say," she explained, "that I actually *met* him, not by design, that is. It was only that he and I both decided quite independently of each other on an early ride, and since the park is almost deserted so early, it was inevitable that we should meet and share the riding paths."

"Yes, my dear, quite inevitable," her aunt answered.

Sarah looked at her aunt inquiringly, but that lady was busy buttering a piece of toast and had on her face such a look of innocence, that she decided her aunt had meant nothing more than to agree with her.

"I think I shall spend the morning at home reading, Aunt Silvia, unless you particularly desire an outing," Sarah commented when they had finished breakfast and were partaking of a second cup of coffee in the Blue Saloon.

"No, no, not at all, love. After last night's ball, and the lateness of the hour at which we retired, a quiet morning at home will suit me very well," the older lady assured her.

However, they were not destined to be alone with their books and stitchery for long. Before much time had passed, Stevens announced Mr. Joshua Brooks.

Mr. Brooks was a tall, slender, elegant gentleman with sandy hair liberally sprinkled with gray. His blue eyes were bright and intelligent. His features were gentle, but his chin showed enough determination that one was not led falsely to believe him to be a weak man. He was by far Sarah's favorite among her suitors, but truth to tell, she looked upon him more as a favorite uncle than a suitor. She had often thought it a shame that either she was not older or he younger, and in spite of the faithfulness of his suit, she could not bring herself to believe that he harbored a tendre for her, but merely the same sort of affection which she felt for him.

Bending gracefully over her hand, Mr. Brooks said in his pleasant voice, "Miss Windemere, I feel myself fortunate indeed to find you at home this morning. It is such a lovely day, I supposed you to be riding in the park."

"I have already had my ride today, sir, and am

very glad I chose to go early. I should have been disappointed to have missed your visit. Let me make you known to my aunt, Mrs. Mashburne. Aunt Silvia, Mr. Brooks is a good friend from home who has come up to London," Sarah answered graciously.

Greeting the gentleman, Mrs. Mashburne asked, "Are you here for the season, sir, or just for a short visit?"

"I shall be here for most of the season," the gentleman answered, "but I fear I shall have to go back on the occasional trip to attend to certain matters concerning my estates. Unfortunately, my old bailiff, a superior man who has been with me for over twenty years, has retired, and the new man is not yet sufficiently familiar with all the details of running the estate to leave alone for long periods of time."

After ringing for refreshments, Sarah inquired into how matters stood with various mutual acquaintances and was assured that everyone was well.

The three engaged in genteel conversation for some thirty minutes, but being a gentleman who adhered strictly to the rules which governed polite society, Mr. Brooks rose to take his leave after the prescribed length of time for a morning call had elapsed, but not before advancing and having accepted an invitation for the two ladies to accompany him to the theater the next evening.

"What a charming gentleman!" Mrs. Mashburne exclaimed when the gentleman had taken his leave of them. "His manners are most pleasing, don't you think so, my dear?"

"Oh, indeed I do," Sarah replied readily. "I have known him these past twelve months, and have grown to like him very much."

"Is he a *particular* suitor of yours?" Mrs. Mashburne asked carefully.

"Oh, good gracious no," Sarah laughed. "I don't hesitate to tell you that we share a mutual liking, and perhaps he would have made me an offer earlier had I encouraged him, but truth to tell, I do not think we would suit at all, and I am quite sure the gentleman has reached the same conclusion and is heartily glad he refrained from declaring himself as soon as my period of mourning was over. He is a perfect dear, and I am sure he will make some lady an excellent husband, but not me."

The slightest blush that tinged her aunt's cheeks did not escape Sarah's notice, and she smiled as she turned to recover the book she had been reading before Mr. Brooks's arrival. Thinking it would be beyond anything wonderful if her dear, gentle aunt and Mr. Brooks should make a match, she was prepared for Mrs. Mashburne's next question.

"I recollect the gentleman is a widower?"

"Yes, for these many years. He has a son who is grown up and married and has children of his own. I think he grows lonely living alone."

"It has been my observation," her aunt commented a trifle too casually, Sarah thought, "that gentlemen frequently do grow lonely when left widowers—much more so than ladies do who lose their husbands. For some reason, ladies seem more able to maintain an establishment and remain contented than men do in similar circumstances, in spite of all the things they must do to govern an estate. Those things simply do not seem to *satisfy* a gentleman the way they do when he is married."

Since almost the exact opposite had been Sarah's observation, she believed her aunt to be looking for hopeful signs that the gentleman in question might be on the lookout for a wife. Not being desirous of putting her aunt to the blush any more than she already was, Sarah declined to comment other than to say that her aunt was very probably right.

Chapter 5

When Mr. Brooks called for the ladies the following evening to accompany them to the theater, he declared himself the most fortunate man in all of London to be escorting the two loveliest ladies in the realm, and indeed it did appear that the ladies had outdone themselves in making themselves attractive for the evening's festivities. Mrs. Mashburne had chosen to wear the new gray crape, which was cut in so simple a style that it took nothing away from her delicate blond beauty, but rather enhanced it. Sarah was wearing a blue watered-silk gown with an open front over a paler blue satin slip. Around her neck and entwined in her hair were diamonds and pearls.

All of London had been raving about Mr. Kean's

performance as Iago at Drury Lane, and he did not disappoint that night's audience.

At intermission, Mr. Brooks asked the ladies if they would like a turn around the theater or perhaps would rather have refreshments sent to their box. Mrs. Mashburne declared that she, for one, would enjoy a stroll, but Sarah declined, saying she had caught the eye of a particular friend of hers and was sure she was coming to the box for a few minutes' conversation before the second act. She asked if they would be kind enough to procure for her a refreshing drink and bring it back with them. Naturally, her aunt agreed, and Sarah soon found herself alone. She had, in fact, seen no good friend, but had made up the tale so that her aunt and Mr. Brooks might have a few minutes alone. She had never in her life played at matchmaking and was finding it rather fun. She only hoped that her aunt would not think she was depriving Sarah of one of her beaux if Mr. Brooks should indeed show a partiality for her. Nothing would please Sarah more than to see her dear aunt happily settled. And Mr. Brooks was *such* a dear.

Upon their return to the box, Sarah was pleased to notice a most becoming blush in her aunt's cheeks and a happy sparkle in her soft blue eyes. Mr. Brooks also was looking uncommonly pleased with himself, and Sarah turned her face away from them to hide a satisfied smile.

Mrs. Mashburne inquired of Sarah if she had had a pleasant coze with her friend, and Sarah was forced to admit that she must have misread her friend's motives, for she had failed to make an appearance, upon which information the older lady at once began to make sincere apologies for leaving Sarah alone.

"For I would never be so inconsiderate, my love, as I am sure you are aware."

"Nonsense," Sarah replied. "To own the truth, I rather enjoyed being alone for a few minutes. Mr. Kean's powerful performance was such that a few reflective moments were welcome. I am so looking forward to the second half. How can we ever thank you enough, Mr. Brooks, for affording us such a rare treat?"

Mrs. Mashburne at once added her thanks to Sarah's, to which Mr. Brooks replied, "You must know, ladies, that the honor and pleasure are all mine. Any number of gentlemen would have been most pleased to escort such lovely ladies and are no doubt at this moment wondering how such a dull dog as I managed to persuade you to accompany me."

The ladies were saved from having to answer by the rising of the curtains. Sarah privately thought that Mr. Brooks was laying it on a trifle too rare and thick, but she could see from the pleased expression on her aunt's face that she was impressed by the gentleman's flowery compliments.

Before saying goodnight to the ladies, Mr. Brooks begged for the pleasure of taking them up for a gentle ride in the park the next afternoon.

"Oh, I *am* sorry, Mr. Brooks," Sarah replied quite mendaciously, "but I have a previous engagement. However," she added, "I don't believe Aunt Silvia is engaged for the afternoon, are you, Aunt? I am sure she would enjoy an outing very much."

"Oh, no, my dear, I shouldn't think of going out without you. It would be much better if I accompanied you on your engagement. I should, of course, enjoy very much a ride in the park, Mr. Brooks, but I am, after all, here as a companion to Sarah."

"Nonsense," Sarah replied. "I am promised to

Lady Ainsberry and haven't the least need for your chaperonage."

Mr. Brooks intervened at that point to say most sincerely that he would be honored if Mrs. Mashburne would consent to accompany him, and that lady, with charming confusion, agreed.

While preparing for bed, Sarah fervently hoped Margaret would be free to receive her the next afternoon, for she in fact had no previous appointment with her. She had no desire to ride in the park with Mr. Brooks, but knew her aunt would enjoy such an outing very much. She was vastly amused at that gentleman's newly discovered silver tongue, for he had never shown to her even the slightest tendency toward flattery. He had, of course, always been attentive and courteous, but as for flattery, no, never. She very much suspected that her gentle aunt was fast making a conquest of her niece's former suitor. Therefore, it was with a great deal of pleasure that Sarah saw her aunt off the following afternoon wearing a lovely gown of sapphire blue and a matching bonnet with dashing ostrich plumes charmingly encircling her golden curls.

Lady Ainsberry was delighted to receive Sarah when she presented herself later in the day. "You must forgive me, dear Margaret, for being so rag-mannered as to call upon you unannounced, but believe me when I tell you that I have the best of reasons."

"I am quite sure you do," laughed Lady Ainsberry, "but surely you know you need no reason to call upon me at any time. I am always pleased to welcome you, as I am sure you must be aware. But come, tell me your news. I can see you are fairly bursting with it."

"You know me too well, Margaret," Sarah retorted

as she made herself comfortable and Lady Ainsberry ordered tea. Then she proceeded to pour into her friend's willing ears her hopes and suspicions concerning her aunt and Mr. Brooks. Lady Ainsberry was quite as pleased as was Sarah and said, "But how charming, dear Sarah. I am only a little acquainted with your aunt, but from the little I have seen of her, she seems to be a most amiable and sweet-natured female, and I wish her every happiness. But forgive me, my friend, if I seem to impose on an old friendship, but was not Mr. Brooks a particular friend of yours? I seem to remember hearing rumors to the effect that an offer of marriage was expected any time these past months and that the gentleman was merely waiting until your period of mourning was over. Am I to understand that an offer would not have been received favorably?"

"Fortunately, Margaret, Mr. Brooks, unlike some others I could mention, is too steeped in the proprieties to make an offer of marriage while one is in mourning, for I am persuaded it would have been a great mistake. I, of course, would have been obliged to refuse him, and that must have put a strain on our friendship. We would not suit, you know, but we *are* good friends, and I would dislike very much for anything to happen to change that agreeable status. For once," she said ruefully, "I am very grateful for the proprieties."

"Poor Sarah," her friend said laughingly, "do you then still chaff against proprieties? I never once feared that you might throw them to the winds, but do remember how you railed against them when we were younger."

"Oh, no, I do not exactly chaff against them *now*. To own the truth, I have reached an age where I can perfectly see the good sense of most of them, but by no means all. My sister, Judith, accuses me of throwing them to the winds, as you put it, by setting up my own establishment, but I do not agree with her at all. If I were a green girl just out of the schoolroom, I could see some justification in her accusations, but surely no one could see the least thing scandalous or even censorious about a woman of my years desiring a home of her own, and to tell the truth, I do not think the ton has taken the least notice of my doings."

"No, nor do I," replied Lady Ainsberry. "At least no one has said anything in my presence. Of course, that could be because it is well known that we are good friends, but I do not think so. You have your aunt to lend you countenance, and I should think that would be as proper as living with your sister."

Changing the subject, Sarah said, "It was shockingly remiss of me not to send around a note thanking you for the lovely evening we all enjoyed so much at your party. I had thought to see you personally before now and thank you, but we have been run almost off our feet these past few days. Please accept my thanks and congratulations now."

"It was a nice party, wasn't it?" Lady Ainsberry agreed. But it's success was dictated more by the sparkle of my guests than anything I might have done. I suppose I could be congratulated upon having the good sense to invite such scintillating people, couldn't I?"

"Don't be a goose," Sarah laughed. "You know well that you are probably the most charming hostess in London."

"Your judgment is clouded by friendship," Margaret replied, pleased nevertheless, "but that does put me in mind of something I wanted to tell you. Do you know my husband is well acquainted with

Ravenwilde and never said one word about it to me until we received that gentleman at the party?"

"No! How could he have been so thoughtless? All the while you were trying to get the man's measure from me, who am barely acquainted with him, your own husband could have given you a wealth of information. Oh, that was really too bad of him," Sarah replied with a twinkle in her eye.

"You laugh, but let me tell you it was no laughing matter with me, as I told Oliver as soon as the last guest had departed," Margaret replied with mock severity. "Tell me, Sarah,"she continued more seriously, "now that you know him a little better, what is your impression?"

"Actually, I do not know him that much better, having encountered him only once or twice since he arrived in London, but I find nothing about the gentleman that would lead me to believe him to be in any way objectionable to the ton. In fact, it is my understanding from his grandmother, who is a great friend of mine, you know, that she is pressuring him to take a wife, so that should make the mamas who have daughters to fire off this season very happy. I very much suspect the gentleman will be welcomed everywhere and only a very few, if any, will remember his earlier peccadilloes."

"Do you then think his exploits were merely that? Peccadilloes, I mean," Lady Ainsberry asked.

"Oh, yes, I am persuaded of it," Sarah replied without hesitation. "His grandmother fairly dotes on him and thinks him, if not a paragon of virtue, certainly a man of honor, and even allowing for a natural partiality the old lady would feel for an only grandson, you must remember that she is a lady of immense character and while she would undoubtedly still love him if he did something really bad, I cannot think she would condone any dishonorable conduct in him or anyone else."

"You are very probably right. When I questioned my husband about him and his past, he merely told me that he had always known Ravenwilde to be a man of character and honor and that he, for one, would completely disregard the rumors concerning him as the jealous exaggerations of a female whose nose had been put out of joint, and that is all I could get Oliver to say on the subject of his friend, except that he would be honored to receive him any time he cared to call and that the two of them had made a luncheon date for the next afternoon. It must have gone well, for they are off today together at some sporting event or another and I do not expect them back until late this afternoon. Oliver did promise to return in time to attend Lady Asher's ball. Do you attend?"

"Yes, my aunt and I received invitations and I am looking forward to it. I collect you will be there, so I will bid you goodbye for now. Perhaps we can all procure a table together at supper, I imagine Mr. Brooks will escort Aunt Silvia and me," she said with a twinkle, "and I am sure you will like him very much."

"That will work out very well," Margaret replied, "for Oliver has promised to take Ravenwilde up in our carriage, and that will even out our numbers."

In the event, however, the numbers were not to be even. No sooner had Sarah and her aunt arrived, escorted by Mr. Brooks, than Ravenwilde solicited Sarah's hand for a dance, begging her in an aside not to refuse him, for he had a favor to ask of her. When they were on the dance floor and had a moment to speak privately, Ravenwilde discreetly pointed out to her a small, lovely young lady with shining blond hair and sea-green eyes and asked her if she was acquainted with her and if so, would she be so good as to introduce her to him. "For she is quite lovely," he said, "and if her background is acceptable, I think my grandmother will approve of her as a prospective wife for me."

Although Sarah again felt that awful sinking feeling in her stomach, she directed a casual glance toward the lady in question and recognized her as Miss Alethia Hampton. Miss Hampton had been the reigning beauty of the season two years past, and while Sarah was not *well* acquainted with her, she did know her slightly and was able to tell his grace that the lady was of impeccable lineage and was held to be a diamond of the first water. She declared that she would be glad to make the introduction.

She then turned the subject to his grandmother, inquiring into her health, and was told that the lady was enjoying excellent health, but was forever prosing on about his need and responsibility to take a wife. "I do not mind telling you, Miss Windemere, that were she not my grandmother, and if I did not hold her in such great respect and affection, I would be strongly tempted to keep my distance, for all she seems to have on her mind these days is a wife for me and an heir in the nursery."

"I am sure your grandmother means well, but she cannot, after all, force you to do something you do not really wish to do," Sarah pointed out to him reasonably.

"No, of course not," his grace agreed, "but the deuce of it is that I realize I have neglected my duty for too long as it is and I cannot but agree with her that it is high time I gave more consideration to what I owe the family."

"Perhaps so," Sarah replied, "but you do not have

to rush into anything. You, after all, are not so old or infirm as to make it a matter of immediate importance."

"No, but as Shakespeare wrote, 'If a thing were done, were best it be done quickly,' or some such thing." Ravenwilde smiled down at her.

Sarah laughed and said, "Yes, *something* like that."

More seriously the duke said, "I doubt it will be too bad. The lady I offer for will be made aware of the fact that ours is to be a marriage of convenience; then if she is willing to accept the few conditions I will be compelled to make, we should deal together well enough."

"I suppose so," Sarah answered, "but I cannot but feel that it is a most unnatural way for one to enter into marriage. However, my feelings on that subject are well known to you, so I will say no more. Each of us must do what he has to do."

"Come, my little innocent, you are as well aware as I that most of the marriages in our society are arranged. The so-called love matches are as rare as they are unsuccessful," the duke pointed out to her.

"Yes, I am sure you are right, which is the reason I shall probably remain in the unmarried state, for I refuse to enter into such a contract without affection," Sarah reiterated.

As soon as the dance ended they made their way to where Miss Hampton was holding court among a number of young gentlemen who had been smitten with her beauty, which, Sarah was forced to admit, was considerable. When the chance arose she said, "Alethia, let me make you known to a newcomer in our midst. This is his grace the Duke of Ravenwilde."

Miss Hampton, ignoring her other suitors, turned limpid green eyes on the duke, and they were soon seen to be well on the way to becoming well acquainted. As soon as Sarah could, she slipped away from the group and joined her aunt and Mr. Brooks.

"It looks to be quite a squeeze, doesn't it, Sarah? Already the heat is almost unbearable. Lady Asher must have thousands of candles lit tonight," her aunt said by way of greeting.

"Yes, to all your comments, dear Aunt. Perhaps you will not want to stay late?" Sarah replied, fervently hoping her aunt would wish to leave early and thus spare her the necessity of watching Ravenwilde and Alethia dancing and talking and laughing together.

She had to admit they made a striking couple. Her delicate blondness made a perfect foil for his tall, dark features, but Sarah, for one, took no pleasure in the handsome picture they made as he twirled the lady around the dance floor. Her only consolation was that the Duchess of Bloomington would be pleased when Ravenwilde reported back to her that he had made the acquaintance of a suitable female.

Far from wanting to leave early, Mrs. Mashburne was having such a good time with Mr. Brooks in attendance that Sarah was forced to abandon that hope and reconcile herself to remaining until the end of the ball. However, she had become so adept at hiding her true feelings that no one was made aware of the fact that she would rather have been anywhere in the world than in the same room with Ravenwilde and Miss Hampton. After a very short while the whole room was alive with the talk of how marked were his grace's attentions to that lovely damsel, and Sarah was obliged to smile and agree that indeed they did make a lovely couple.

Due to Sarah's undoubted popularity, she was

never left for long without an escort, and it was becoming more difficult by the minute to smile and display the charm for which she was justly famous. Hoping for a repast of some duration, she was very glad when it came time to go down for supper, but it was Miss Hampton whom Ravenwilde escorted down and not Sarah as Lady Ainsberry had so fondly planned. Sarah had declined all invitations to escort her, and the numbers, as Lady Ainsberry had tried to prevent, were not even. However, since everyone was fairly well acquainted with everyone else, the supper time was not so bad as it might have been, that is, except for Sarah. Her breeding and good manners prevented her from allowing anyone to see how very miserable she really was, and the time passed quite merrily for the rest of the company. Even her aunt was too engrossed with Mr. Brooks to notice that anything was amiss with Sarah, a circumstance for which that young lady was devoutly thankful.

However, in thinking her blue mood had passed completely unremarked, she was wrong. As soon as the party had again assembled in the ball room, Ravenwilde solicited Sarah's hand for the waltz that was just at that moment striking up. She wanted very much to refuse, but knew she could not without making an explanation, and that she could not do.

"What has happened to overset you, my dear?" he asked as soon as they were twirling gracefully across the floor. "And don't tell me nothing, for I can see very well that something has."

Startled, Sarah raised her eyes to his, and seeing the warm concern there, she almost missed a step. Ravenwilde tightened his hold around her waist, drawing her even closer to him, and she hastily lowered her lashes. "Actually, it isn't anything more than a slight headache," she replied somewhat breathlessly. "It is much too warm. I think Lady Asher must have bought all the candles in London for this night."

"Are you sure that is all?" he asked her softly. "You surely know you can rely upon me should you need a friend, or confidant. You can even cry on my shoulder if you like," he finished teasingly.

"Oh, sir, that is friendship indeed. Remember, you have ruined the front of your shirt with women's tears," Sarah answered, the twinkle returning to her eyes.

"That's much better," Ravenwilde said. "It was the twinkle missing from your lovely eyes that tipped me off to the fact that something was not quite right with you. I shouldn't like it to be spread abroad that I offered, but I would gladly offer my chest if you ever feel the need to weep."

"But I couldn't do that," Sarah answered with a mischievous smile. "You see, I am not one of those fortunate few who can cry prettily. My eyes and nose turn red and my face breaks out in horrible red splotches. No, your grace, crying is a luxury I simply cannot afford."

"I cannot believe that," he answered, returning a mischievous smile of his own. "I am persuaded you do *everything* charmingly."

"Flummery, sir. I think you offer me Spanish coin," she answered.

"You wound me, little one. That I should never do. I value your friendship too much." And so saying, he again tightened his hold on her, thus drawing her even closer still, until she was very much afraid their closeness would cause remark. The duke must have had the same fear, for he immediately loosened his hold and they finished the dance in silence.

"I visit your grandmother tomorrow," Sarah informed him as they were leaving the floor. "May I carry a message for you?"

"I thank you, no, for I am engaged to call upon her tomorrow myself. Oh, by the by," he added, "I am also engaged to ride in the park with Miss Hampton tomorrow. I failed to thank you for introducing me to her."

"I hope you never have cause to regret it," Sarah answered, but since her words were accompanied by a smile, the duke chose to accept them lightly.

"Life being what it is, I've no doubt I *shall* regret it on occasion, but be assured, I shall never blame you."

"You relieve my mind, your grace," she answered with false sweetness.

"Vixen," he replied with a smile.

The evening finally ended, and Sarah was left alone (after having to listen to her aunt's rapturous recollections for some thirty minutes) to sink wearily into her bed. The headache she had assured Ravenwilde to be the cause of her out-of-common moping had become a reality, and she lay for quite some time suffering not only from the pain in her head, but also from a peculiar constriction in the region of her heart. She berated herself for being all kinds of a fool, a widgeon, and acting like a silly schoolroom miss. Indeed, she assured herself, she had never acted like a schoolroom miss even when she *was* one, and here she was seven and twenty letting things that were no bread and butter of hers throw her into a fit of the dismals. Well, tomorrow would bring a new dawn, and she would put all these cares behind her and enjoy the remainder of the season.

She had already determined that this would be her last season, or at least her last *complete* season.

She might come to London for a particular ball or party or to do some shopping, but she would not endure another whole season. For some reason, this season, to which she had looked forward with so much pleasure, had this night become tedious. Oh, she enjoyed seeing her old friends, but surely one did not have to endure the routs, balls, and dinners in order to have a visit with one's friends.

Suddenly the thoughts of home, the country, and the small estate that was hers were very inviting, and she determined to send a message the very next day to the servants there to make the house ready for her return. She might not even remain in London for the whole of the season. These thoughts had a soporific effect, and soon Sarah was able to drift into a deep and dreamless sleep.

When she awoke the next morning, there was still a trace of the headache but not nearly so bad as it had been the night before. A critical look into her mirror revealed the ravages of pain and a mostly sleepless night. There were dark circles under her swollen eyes, and her lips were pinched and pale. There was no color at all in her cheeks. One look at her pale and pinched countenance was enough to throw her aunt into a worried flutter. She first inquired if Sarah was sickening for something; a cold, perhaps, or a disorder of the stomach. Had she eaten something at Lady Asher's ball that could have overset her stomach? She knew full well that that starchiest of ladies would be reduced to spasms if it were merely hinted that she had served her guests anything that might sicken them. Upon being told that none of these things were the cause of her malady, but that she suspected she was merely overtired, Mrs. Mashburne immediately began to chastise herself for not taking better care of her beloved Sarah.

It was, after all, her duty and indeed her pleasure to see that no harm came to her niece, and remembering that Sarah had actually suggested that they might leave the ball early, she began such a litany of self-reproach that it took Sarah quite some ten minutes to calm her.

"For you surely know, you lovely pea goose, that had I not been feeling well last night, I could have made my excuses at any time. You need not have left with me, you know, for surely our own dear John Coachman would have been ample escort."

"But, my dear, Mr. Brooks escorted us to the ball," Mrs. Mashburne pointed out to her. "We didn't have our own coach with us."

"Yes, to be sure, I had forgotten," Sarah answered, leaning her elbows on the table and supporting her head. "Well, no matter, I am sure I could have contrived a way home had I felt the need. The fact is, I did not feel the need, and this miserable headache is simply the result of my racketing around town too much and being overheated last night. My own fault, love, and not to be laid at your door."

"But, my dear Sarah..."

"We'll say no more on that head, if you please," Sarah interrupted, "but I should be glad if you will send a message around to the Duchess of Bloomington telling her that I am slightly indisposed and expressing my regrets that I will be unable to call upon her as planned this morning."

"Of course, my dear, and anything else you might wish me to do that might in any way add to your comfort. While I am about it, I will send a message also to Mr. Brooks canceling my ride in the park with him this afternoon."

"You'll do no such thing!" Sarah answered with some asperity. "I am not an invalid who needs constant attention. I am merely a little overtired, and I cannot imagine what you could do to alleviate that condition. I shall be much better off if left alone to rest in my room. There is not the slightest need for you to change any plans you may have made for your enjoyment, and indeed, I shall rest much easier knowing that my silly indisposition is not causing you any inconvenience. Now, please, love, don't argue with me, for arguing only makes my wretched head ache even more. I think I shall have a fresh pot of tea sent to my room. After a bath, I shall very probably go back to bed for the rest of the day. I know I can depend upon you to see that I am not disturbed."

"Of course, my dear. Are you sure there is nothing I can do for you?" Mrs. Mashburne asked solicitously.

"Oh, yes, quite sure. No, there is one thing. I should consider it a kindness if you would not spread it abroad that I am not feeling well. You know how I particularly detest having people fawn over me. Besides being bothered by those who might feel it their duty to visit me, when I do go out again, I should be obliged to answer all manner of questions concerning my health and the reasons for my indisposition. It is only a small thing, you know, and I would much prefer not to have it remarked upon."

Mrs. Mashburne readily agreed to this, and the ladies parted, each to her own bedchamber.

Chapter 6

After spending a quiet hour drinking her tea and trying not to think, Sarah rang for a maid and requested that a bath be prepared. She felt much refreshed after the bath, but decided to lie down for a while anyway.

Much to her surprise, it was almost the dinner hour when she awoke, and upon being advised that her aunt was out for the evening, she decided upon a cold repast for herself. She was taking her coffee in the book room when Stevens, after a discreet knock on the door, asked her if she was at home to callers.

Much surprised, she asked, "Now who on earth would be calling at this time of night? No, Stevens, I cannot receive. Please deny me."

But before that superior gentleman could carry out his mistress's wishes, the Duke of Ravenwilde pushed his way into the room. "Nonsense, Sarah, it is only I and you needn't stand on ceremony with me. Good God," he exclaimed when he was close enough to see her clearly, "what the devil have you been doing to yourself? You look completely knocked up."

Laughing in spite of herself, Sarah said, "Oh, that is too bad of you, Ravenwilde. Do I really look so bad?"

Taking her chin into his hand and turning her head toward the light, he answered, "No, not bad. Nothing, I am persuaded, could make you look *bad*, but you do look a trifle under the weather. I knew last night, my girl, that you were not feeling all the thing. Come, sit down and tell me all about it."

"Oh, there really isn't anything to tell, your grace," and turning to Stevens, who was watching with a great deal of interest, she asked that he be good enough to bring refreshments for his grace.

When they were along again, Ravenwilde took her hand in his and said, "Now I insist, tell me what ails you. Have you had the doctor? Where is your aunt? Surely she has not left you alone?"

"Don't be a goose, Ravenwilde. Of course she has left me alone and no, I have not had the doctor. I am just a little tired, that's all. I think the excessive heat last night caused me to have the headache, which, I assure you, is a thing I seldom do. But tell me, how did you know I was not well? I particularly asked Aunt Silvia not to mention it."

"It was not your aunt but my grandmother who informed me. She told me you had cried off today because of a slight indisposition, as she put it. I had thought it might be a passing thing, but when I

arrived at Lady Blackburne's ball, which you specifically said you would attend, and found you ab-
sent, I came around to check. Your aunt was no doubt
there, but I could not locate her in the crowd. God,
what an awful squeeze! My grandmother was very
much concerned about you, for she told me she could
never remember your being sick in all the years she
has known you."

"Well, and I am not sick now," Sarah replied,
trying unsuccessfully to remove her hand from his
grasp, but he would not release her until Stevens
returned with the tray of drinks.

"Enough about me," Sarah said when they were
once again alone. "Tell me, how does your suit with
Miss Hampton prosper?"

"Predictably, I suppose," he answered with a no-
ticeable lack of enthusiasm. "We rode in the park
today and I am committed to escorting her to Vauxhall Gardens tomorrow night. My grandmother professes to be pleased. I do not know how she contrives
to stay at home and still be aware of all the things
that are going on in town. Someone had already been
before me in telling her about my attentions to Miss
Hampton; my *marked* attentions is the way she put
it."

"And indeed they were marked," Sarah replied.
"The whole room was alive with talk of it. You know,
of course, and can admit it to me without fear that
I will think you conceited, that you are the prize
catch of the season, and Miss Hampton is considered
to be quite a beauty."

"I suppose she is a pretty little thing," the duke
conceded.

"Pretty little thing, indeed!" Sarah retorted. "She
is considered to be a diamond of the first water, a
pearl past price, a—"

"Enough," he laughed. "I will admit that she is a great beauty, but the lady is just a mite insipid, don't you think?"

"Well," Sarah temporized, "I cannot say that I am *that* well acquainted with her. You know I was not here last season, and the season before was her come-out. One really cannot judge girls on the performance of their first season. Too often they are thrown into the ton without the least notion of how to go on, and I have always thought it most unkind to hold them so much accountable for their actions their first season."

"Ah, dear Sarah, but you are not unkind." The Duke smiled at her. "You must admit, however, that the majority of the ton is made up of gabble gabbers and scandal mongers who are waiting like so many vultures for someone to make a false move."

After a short time which was filled with more conversation along those same lines, Ravenwilde took his leave of her, promising to return the next day, and Sarah took herself off to bed feeling very much better.

When she joined her aunt the next morning for breakfast, she was feeling and looking much more herself than when that lady had last seen her. "Oh, my love," Mrs. Mashburne exclaimed, "how glad I am to see you looking so well. I must admit to have been excessively worried about you last evening and would never have gone out except that I knew you would be vexed had I stayed at home to play nurse-maid. However, I really should have stayed home, for I fear I was very poor company."

"I doubt Mr. Brooks would agree with you, Aunt," Sarah retorted with a twinkle in her eyes.

"Oh, no," Mrs. Mashburne replied, blushing rosily. "When I tried to apologize for my poor company, he said all that was gracious and assured me that he quite understood the situation. He is a man of great sensibilities, Sarah, and I cannot but wonder that you did not appreciate him more."

"It is not that I do not appreciate that he is a worthy gentleman, nor that I am insensible to the honor he paid me by his attentions. Indeed, I know him to be a gentleman of the first stare. It is merely that he and I would not suit, and fortunately, we both came to realize that melancholy truth before it was too late. Now that you know the gentleman better, dearest Aunt, tell the truth—can you imagine the two of us married? I should drive the poor man to murder in less than six months."

"Never say so, my love, for he is much too kind and gentle to resort to *murder*," Mrs. Mashburne replied with a twinkle of her own, "but I must admit, it would have been a hard go for both of you."

"Exactly so," replied Sarah wryly.

"But tell me truthfully, Sarah," Mrs. Mashburne asked worriedly, "are you perfectly sure you do not resent Mr. Brooks's squiring me all over town? I shudder to think what Judith will have to say when news of this reaches her ears, and depend upon it, she *will* hear of it, if she has not already done so."

"Rest easy, Aunt. If I cared a groat for what Judith thinks, I should still be living with her. As for how I feel personally, I never wanted Mr. Brooks for either a suitor or a husband. I value his friendship, and hope that I can always count him as a friend. But tell me, has he made an offer?"

"No, nor have I encouraged him to think one would be received with favor," her aunt answered slowly and a little sadly.

"Why ever not?" Sarah asked, much astonished.

"It is as plain as the nose on your pretty face that you are in love with him."

"Oh, please do not say so," begged the older lady, much discomfited. "Have I been making a spectacle of myself?"

"Of course not, you pretty goose," Sarah answered, reaching across the table to take her aunt's hand in her own. "It is just that I know you so well. Now tell me, why have you not encouraged Mr. Brooks? Surely you can see he returns your affections."

"Oh, Sarah, my love. You know I could never leave you. What would you do? You certainly do not want to go back to Judith, and I know you would never consider living alone. Why, even *I* could not approve that. You must have a respectable, older female to lend you countenance. What an ungrateful wretch I should be if I should even consider for a moment abandoning you!" Tears had welled up in the lady's blue eyes, but she was striving to keep them from overflowing.

"Now you are being foolish beyond permission, Aunt Silvia," Sarah replied severely. "You yourself said there are any number of ladies who would be glad to stand in your shoes. While I do not really think there are *that* many, I am sure we could find *one* respectable female to companion me. At any rate, I doubt you would marry before the end of the season, and I have already determined that this is to be my final season. In fact, I have already written to advise the servants to hold Foxborough in readiness, for I mean to return there at the season's end. Indeed, I may return before. Somehow, being in London is not as exciting or as satisfying as it once was," she said rather wistfully, but continued in more rallying tones, "And you know, my brother and his wife live so close that I probably will not need a chaperon at all. If I do need one, there are any number of ladies in the neighborhood who will be glad to accompany me on an outing, I assure you. Now, we'll have no more of this nonsense. All that is necessary is that you make up your own mind what you want to do and do it without the least consideration for *my* well-being, for I do assure you, I shall be fine."

Mrs. Mashburne was spared the necessity of answering by Stevens announcing, in a tone that told Sarah he disapproved of early callers, the Duke of Ravenwilde.

"Stevens tried to keep me out, Sarah, but I assured him that I would not take more than a few minutes of your time and that I had warned you that I would be dropping by this morning," Ravenwilde said in his usual candid manner.

"Yes, you did, but I really did not expect you so early. Have you had breakfast?" Sarah asked with only a slight twitch at the corners of her mouth.

"Yes," he answered, "but I should be glad of another cup of coffee, if I am not intruding." Turning to Mrs. Mashburne, he dazzled her with a singularly sweet smile and was assured by both ladies that he was welcome to share their coffee.

"I am glad to see you looking so much better this morning," he told Sarah while giving her face a thorough scrutiny with his keen eyes. "I do not mind telling you that you looked fagged to death last night."

"I wonder, sir, if there is anything you *would* mind telling me," Sarah replied with false sweetness.

Ravenwilde appeared to give this careful consideration before answering seriously, "No, I don't think there is."

"Wretch," Sarah answered, unsuccessfully trying to suppress the gurgle of laughter in her throat.

"That's better, my girl," Ravenwilde smiled approvingly.

While Ravenwilde and Sarah bantered back and forth in this fashion, Mrs. Mashburne watched and sipped her coffee. She was amazed at the familiarity between the two, and even more so as she observed and heard the free and easy exchange between them. Could it be that they were forming a tendre for each other?

She noticed the sparkle in Sarah's eyes as she laughed at some remark of Ravenwilde's and the softening of his features as he studied her face. She really had not been attending to what was being said between them but was lost in her speculations as to what such a match would mean when Sarah turned to her and said, "I think it would be most diverting, don't you, Aunt Sarah?"

"I am sorry, my dear, I was not attending. What do you think would be diverting?"

"Ravenwilde is taking Miss Hampton to Vauxhall Gardens tonight and proposes to make a party of it. He has already asked his grandmother and she has consented to make one of the party. Mr. and Mrs. Hampton and a nephew who is recuperating from a war injury will also be along. He has now invited us. What do you think?"

"Oh, my dear, I am sure it would be most enjoyable, but I am engaged to Lady Langly tonight for a small dinner party. Of course, if you *particularly* want to go to Vauxhall, I shall cry off."

"Nonsense! There is no need for that. With the duchess there to act as chaperon, there is no need for you to go if you have already accepted another invitation. Nothing could be more unexceptionable than the Duchess of Bloomington's chaperonage.

Even the highest stickler could find nothing to remark about *that*."

"Certainly not," Mrs. Mashburne agreed at once, "but I am, after all, supposed to be your chaperon, and I am very sure that Judith would not approve of your going places without me."

"I think we have already established the fact that I care naught for what Judith likes or dislikes. The party will be most unexceptionable, and I wouldn't for a moment want you to change your plans to suit mine. After all, you did not know I would even be well enough to go out tonight."

"That is true, love, and to be quite honest with you, I did not expect you to be. I know you will not take it amiss if I tell you that I agree with his grace that you were not looking at all well yesterday, and since you are *never* ill, I feared you were sickening for something far worse than you were willing to admit." Turning to Ravenwilde, she explained with her charming smile, "You may wonder, sir, that I planned to go out thinking that Sarah would not be well, but you must know that of all things she dislikes to be fussed over. If we are not to come to cuffs, I am forced to ignore any slight indisposition of hers."

"No need to explain to me, Mrs. Mashburne. I think I have known the lady long enough to have a fair understanding and measure of her character. She is, in fact, much too independent for her own good."

"I do beg your pardons," Sarah said with considerable hauteur, "but I would appreciate it very much if you would not discuss me as if I were not here. Aunt Silvia may know me very well, but as for you, Ravenwilde, it surpasses my understanding how you can claim so deep an understanding of my character after so short an acquaintance."

"Frankly, my dear," he answered seriously but with a twinkle in his eyes to which Sarah could not help responding, "it surpasses mine as well, but so it is. Some things simply cannot be explained rationally."

"Blabberdash," Sarah replied, most unladylike.

"Before you fly up into the boughs, I think we should finalize our plans for the evening. My grandmother and I will take you up in my carriage at eight o'clock and proceed on to Miss Hampton's home, if that meets with your approval?"

"Of course. I shall look forward to seeing you and especially the duchess. She is quite my favorite person, you know."

"Yes, I do know," he replied, smiling, "and you may be sure she holds you in the same affection as you hold her."

"Yes, I know," Sarah said, "and greatly feel the honor."

The duke soon took his leave of the ladies, and even though Sarah insisted she felt perfectly well, she did consent to spend a quiet day at home and instructed Stevens that she was not at home to callers.

In order that Mrs. Mashburne might not be denied the pleasure of receiving any callers whom she might wish to see, Sarah took herself off to her own rooms, where she stayed until time for lunch. Afterward she again retired to her bedchamber, where she spent the greater part of the afternoon deciding just which gown and accessories to wear that evening. If her maid thought it strange (and she did), she did not comment when Miss Windemere, who was always so decisive and sure about what was right for any occasion, hesitated and agonized over whether to wear the blue silk or the rose crepe, or maybe even the green jersey—but no, the jersey simply would not do, for she didn't like it above half and didn't Sally think the hem of the blue silk sagged just the tiniest bit on the left side? No, clearly the blue silk would not do at all until the offending hem was adjusted, so perhaps the navy twill? But no, again. It would simply have to be the rose crepe. Everything else was either too formal or not formal enough, or as in the case of the green, the blue, and the navy, offended in some other way. However, hadn't she worn the rose crepe at least twice already this season? Suddenly her vast wardrobe seemed positively shabby!

By the time Sarah had settled on what to wear and how her hair was to be arranged, it was time for her bath, and when, a minute or two before eight, she floated out of her room and down the stairs, a perfect vision in a pale beige silk gown with a darker brown overskirt and a Norwich silk shawl around her white shoulders, her maid was left to wonder what on earth had come over miss!

Promptly at eight, Ravenwilde was ushered into the hall just in time to see Sarah float down the last few steps, holding out her hands in greeting and bestowing upon him a warm smile.

"Ah, Ravenwilde, on time I see," she said.

"Whatever are my faults, my dear, keeping a lovely lady waiting is not one of them," he answered, smiling.

"And I shouldn't think you would relish keeping your grandmother waiting, either," Sarah replied mischievously.

"Just so," he answered dryly.

The duchess greeted Sarah warmly when Ravenwilde helped her into the carriage. "You look lovely, my dear," the older lady said, "but then you always do. It has always amazed me how you manage to set the standard by which every other lady in a room is judged."

"Please, ma'am," Sarah laughed, "you make me sound like a female Brummell."

Since Miss Hampton resided not far from Sarah, the carriage soon stopped again, and while Ravenwilde went inside to fetch the lady, the duchess took the opportunity to ask Sarah what she thought about her.

"Really, ma'am, I hardly know how to answer. I am not that well acquainted with Miss Hampton. As you know, I was not in town last season, and the season before that was Miss Hampton's come-out. To tell the truth, I did not pay much attention to her, but I remember her as a prettily behaved child. If her mama was a bit pushy, well, who can blame her? I understand she has four younger daughters to fire off, and that must be a burden for any mother."

"Well," answered her grace, "I remember her as a dead bore, but then, I find most extremely young persons boring. Of course, I don't include *you* in that category, my dear, as you well know."

"But then I am not an *extremely young* person, am I?" Sarah teased.

"No," replied the older lady with a slight smile, "you are an impertinent piece of baggage."

The two ladies were laughing as Ravenwilde opened the carriage door and handed Miss Hampton into it. After the ladies had greeted each other, Ravenwilde said, "Are you two going to let us in on the joke, or was it private?"

"Not at all," Sarah answered. "Your grandmother was just telling me what a shameless bit of baggage she thinks me."

"Oh, no, Miss Windemere," Miss Hampton exclaimed in shocked tones. "I am persuaded you must have misunderstood her grace."

"I assure you I did not," Sarah answered. "The duchess and I have a perfect understanding."

"Oh," replied Miss Hampton, settling as far back into the seat as possible, apparently fearing that the two ladies were on the verge of verbal conflict.

Correctly reading Miss Hampton's thoughts, Sarah fought to suppress a gurgle of laughter, but meeting Ravenwilde's eyes, the laughter died in her throat and she almost gasped when she saw him smiling at her with such sweetness. But it was the strange expression she saw in his eyes that caused her to catch her breath. Later she told herself that she had misread the look he was bestowing upon her and convinced herself that the failing light had been responsible.

Vauxhall Gardens was enjoying a renewed burst of popularity, and the grounds were already crowded when they arrived. Ravenwilde made a path for them among the assorted classes of people who had decided upon the gardens for that night's entertainment. Riffraff rubbed shoulders with members of the ton, and Ravenwilde was anxious to escort his ladies to the booth he had hired, which looked out onto the crowded dance floor and in which Miss Hampton's parents and cousin were already settled.

Mr. Hampton was a large, affable gentleman who was universally liked and good-naturedly teased by other gentlemen for being the only male in a large household of females. This teasing he took in good part, for he was an affectionate, if somewhat careless, father who left the rearing of his daughters in the capable hands of his wife. When that lady ventured to seek his advice, he invariably suggested that she do whatever she deemed best, saying, "For

I know nothing about rearing females," and adding in such tones of painful regret that they never failed to make his wife feel guilty, "Now if only I had had a son..." thus ensuring that she would not burden him again for many weeks with anything concerning the girls or her own fears for their future.

The truth of the matter was that he never seriously regretted not having a son. After all, though he was well off enough to provide for his family and even bestow upon each of his daughters a respectable, if not generous, dowry, he was not the possessor of *great* wealth and estates, or even a minor title which would render a male heir desirable. He was a sporting gentleman, but being acquainted with a number of other gentlemen of like persuasion, he never lacked for male companionship. In truth, he was often glad that the responsibilities of guiding the growth and education of a son had not befallen him.

Mrs. Hampton was a small, birdlike woman who looked fragile but was actually as indomitable a lady as ever stormed the citadels of the ton. With five daughters to marry off eligibly, and an indifferent husband who could not even be persuaded to introduce into the house the sons of any of his acquaintances, she had a formidable task. She had early realized the magnitude of her responsibility and had been planning her strategy for many years. Now it seemed that she was on the verge of a greater success than she would have imagined even in her wildest dreams, for none other than the Duke of Ravenwilde was paying court to her eldest daughter. Who would ever have thought that she would be sharing a box at Vauxhall with the dowager Duchess of Bloomington? Of course, she could not like it that Miss Windemere also shared that box, and was on *such* intimate terms with the duchess, but the girl (if one could call her a girl) must be all of seven and twenty—clearly not in her first bloom. However, one had to admit that she was still a striking lady, and she wondered petulantly why her own daughters could not have just a particle of the charm which Miss Windemere possessed in such abundance. Ah, well, Ravenwilde could not be interested in a female so long in the tooth. Her own little girl had the advantages of innocence, youth, and a certain blond beauty which Miss Windemere could not lay claim to.

Miss Hampton's cousin, Mr. Leghorne, was a slightly built young man with pale complexion and regular features. His blue eyes looked at the world with a weary tolerance, but when he bestowed his rare smile upon one, it was seen to light up his whole face. His blond hair had a tendency to fall forward onto his forehead, and he occasionally swept it back with a white, slender, beautifully graceful hand. Sarah wondered how such a frail, aesthetic-looking gentleman had ever become a soldier, and at the first opportunity commented upon that fact to Ravenwilde, who smiled slightly and answered, "You would be surprised, my dear, how deceptive looks can be in actual battle. Why, I have seen—"

But he broke off abruptly, causing Sarah to look at him quizzingly and ask, "Yes, Ravenwilde, what have you seen?"

"Nothing, how could I? Please forget I said anything so foolish. You must know I am known to occasionally ramble on to no purpose."

Much to Sarah's disappointment, their conversation was interrupted by Mrs. Hampton's calling Ravenwilde's attention to some small matter, and had Sarah not been too engrossed in what he had inadvertently let slip, she would have been amused at that lady's obvious attempt to distract Ravenwilde's attentions from her.

Ravenwilde asked both of the younger ladies if they cared to dance, but both were reluctant to rub shoulders with the truly amazing assortment of people enjoying the dance floor, and they declined. Mr. Leghorne excused himself from begging their hands for a dance on the grounds of his indifferent health, and indeed it was seen that that gentleman was still weak and favored his left leg over the right.

Ravenwilde had ordered supper for later, but for the time being, the party was content to watch the dancers and those milling around the grounds. They saw several people they knew and exchanged smiles and nods. Occasionally an acquaintance would drop by to remark surprise and pleasure at seeing the duchess at Vauxhall and to cast meaningful glances in the direction of Ravenwilde and Miss Hampton.

Mrs. Hampton soon noticed an old and favorite friend occupying the box almost directly across from Ravenwilde's and invited the whole party to accompany her to pay a visit so that she might make them all known to dear Lady Oxford. The duchess declined, giving as her excuse that she was an old woman and too much gallivanting around would overly tire her. Casting her a private and amused smile, Sarah declared that she would remain in the box to keep the duchess company and urged the rest of the party not to give them another thought.

"Really, ma'am," Sarah teased when they were alone, "you quite took the pleasure out of the expedition for her. *You* were the grand prize to be displayed before her old friend."

"Yes, I know," the older lady answered with a twinkle in her clear blue eyes, "but you know how

I hate that sort of thing. The Hampton woman is too clever to be obviously encroaching, and even though I sympathize with her problems, I cannot like her. She lacks a certain delicacy of conduct that one expects in a lady of quality, don't you agree?"

"As always, ma'am, I bow to your superior judgment," Sarah replied. "However, I see nothing displeasing in *Miss* Hampton's conduct. She is a trifle shy and perhaps too lacking in conversation for my taste, but that very thing which I perceive as a fault is considered by many to be a virtue."

The ladies found themselves in agreement on this and other subjects that arose and spent an enjoyable time together having an agreeable coze until suddenly the old lady stiffened. Sarah, sensing that something was troubling her, took one of her hands (which she was shocked to find was icy cold) into her own and looked into her pale face. "What is it, ma'am? What has happened to overset you? Are you ill? Shall I call Ravenwilde to take you home?"

"No, no, my dear," the duchess replied. "It is nothing, merely the shock of seeing Harry's cousin."

"Cousin?" Sarah said, perplexed. "Where? I knew he had a cousin, of course, but I did not know he was in town. He is Ravenwilde's heir, isn't he?"

"Yes, more's the pity. A gamester and a waster, as brass-faced as they come. I had heard he was in town, but this is the first time I have seen him. Naturally we would not encounter him in the *normal* way, for he is not received, you know. He has been living on his expectations as Harry's heir these many years, and it has reached my ears that he was none too pleased to learn that Harry was back in England. He is a bad man, Sarah; I have even at times fancied him to be an evil man."

"Oh, no, ma'am," Sarah answered, shocked. "Surely you worry unnecessarily."

"Perhaps," the old lady answered, clearly unconvinced. "Here he comes now; he has spotted us. I am sorry for it, my dear, but I shall be forced to present you to him."

"Never mind, ma'am," she replied with mirth lurking in her lovely eyes. "Surely together our credit must stand being seen in the company of such as he for a few minutes, especially since he is in some way related."

"Not to me, he isn't," the duchess retorted just as the gentleman in question strode up, making it necessary for Sarah to conceal her vast amusement.

He was a small man with dark, almost black, piercing eyes and black hair. His dress proclaimed him to be of the dandy set, or at least an imitator of that set, and when he bent over Sarah's hand and brushed it with his moist, flaccid lips, she felt a shiver of revulsion race down her back and chided herself for letting the duchess's words influence her so. However, in all honesty, she told herself, there was something oily about the man and she could not like him.

"Ah, finally I have the pleasure and honor of meeting the beautiful Miss Windemere," he said smoothly, studying her features. "But you are more beautiful than I had been led to believe."

"You flatter me, sir," Sarah replied coolly.

"Not at all, Miss Windemere. I only say what I see with my own two eyes."

Sarah refused to honor with an answer what she felt to be gross and unwarranted flattery from a complete stranger, and so the gentleman turned to the dowager duchess. "And you, your grace, are looking younger every season."

"Flummery," that gracious lady replied, and Sarah

hid a smile behind her fan. "But tell me, Donnelly, what brings you to town?"

"Why, the season, of course, ma'am," he replied, faking surprise. "What else?"

"I really do not know," she answered shortly. "That is why I asked."

"But you must know I spend a part of every season in London," he replied smoothly, refusing to take offense, "and this year I was compelled to come whether I wanted to or not. I understand my cousin has returned from his voyages, and I felt it my duty to welcome him home and to ascertain if there is any way I might be of service. He has been away so long that there must be any number of small services I might render. I daresay he is a stranger in many quarters after so long an absence."

"I believe he goes on very well," the duchess answered, "but here he comes now. You may ask him yourself."

After making his cousin known to the rest of the party, Ravenwilde escorted him out of the box, where they spent some few minutes in conversation. It was not known what they discussed, and when Ravenwilde reentered the box none of the party except the duchess and Sarah was aware that he was not in his usual good humor. However, those two ladies were quick to notice the tightness of his jaw and the steady beat of his pulse at the base of his jaw just above his collar. His eyes, too, were hard and the smile on his lips was forced.

Exchanging glances, Sarah and the duchess, by mutual and unspoken agreement, endeavored to turn the attention of the party away from him until he had had time to restore his equanimity. Being a man of even temper, this was soon accomplished, and at the first opportunity, he silently thanked the two ladies with a secret smile and, in Sarah's case at least, a quick squeeze of her hand.

Chapter 7

When Ravenwilde went to sit beside Miss Hampton, Sarah found herself more or less alone with Mr. Leghorne and enjoyed some twenty minutes of his gentle conversation. However, she could not help but notice the frequency with which his eyes strayed to the corner of the box which was occupied by Ravenwilde and Miss Hampton and wondered if the unfortunate young man had formed an attachment for his pretty cousin. Pity the poor man if he had, for Mrs. Hampton would never approve such a match. Clearly she had her sights set on bigger game!

After an early supper, Ravenwilde suggested that Sarah and Miss Hampton accompany him on a walk around the gardens, ending at a spot which would afford them a better view of the fireworks display that was promised for later. Mr. Leghorne was included in the invitation but declined because of his lame leg. After making sure that the two older ladies were comfortable, the three set off down one of the numerous paths that marked the gardens.

They had not gone far when Sarah heard running footsteps behind them and, turning to see who it might be, caught a glimpse of someone emerging from the bushes to the side of them. She had no time to notice anything else before one of the two rough-looking men who had suddenly confronted them grabbed Ravenwilde and the other rudely pushed Miss Hampton and herself to the side. One of the men was holding Ravenwilde from behind while the other was advancing holding a gleaming instrument threateningly in one upraised hand.

The man holding Ravenwilde in a crushing grip hissed, "'urry up, we ain't got all night, you know."

"Are you sure this be the right cove?" the other growled in return.

"Course I'm sure. 'e's the right one, allright. Now 'urry."

Sarah's first impulse was to run for help, but she realized almost immediately that there was no time. She looked around for a weapon—a rock, a stick, anything—but could find nothing. She had left her reticule with the duchess and carried only her fan, a fragile looking thing, but one with webs of ivory holding the lovely pieces of silk together. Realizing there was not much she could do against the man holding the knife, she advanced on the one holding Ravenwilde and began stabbing him in the side with the closed fan, using all the strength she could muster. He immediately let out a curse and loosened his hold on Ravenwilde just enough for that gentleman to break loose. With a strength that amazed the onlooking Sarah, Ravenwilde flung the man aside just in time to check the arm of the knife-wielding attacker. After that everything became blurred for Sarah in a haze of flaying arms and muted groans and curses. Sensing a movement at her side, she turned in time to see the first attacker lunge for Ravenwilde and instinctively thrust out one delicately shod foot and tripped the man as he made a rush to pass her. He fell to the ground with a grunt, and it took all the willpower Sarah possessed not to cry out from the pain in her ankle when the large man's leg collided with her smaller one.

Getting heavily to his feet, the first attacker shouted, "Come on, let's get out of 'ere. I 'ear somebody coming."

Hearing these words, the second man ceased his struggles with Ravenwilde and ran in the opposite direction from the first.

Sarah ran to Ravenwilde and clutching his arm said, "Are you all right?" He did not cut you with the knife, did he?"

"No, I am all right," he said as he bent over and picked up the knife his assailant had dropped. Together he and Sarah examined it. "A wicked-looking piece, isn't it?"

"Yes," she agreed, "and for a moment there I thought it would surely be buried in your heart."

"And it very probably would have been had you not entered the fray. I should give you a thundering scold, but I haven't the heart for it, particularly since you saved my life. All I can do is render you my most humble thanks."

"Nonsense. Anyone would have done the same," she replied in rallying tones.

"And you, are you all right?" he asked belatedly.

"Yes, except for a little pain in my ankle I am

afraid it might have suffered a slight bruise when I tripped one of our friends when he would attack you from behind again. Oh, infamous! How can anyone be so cowardly?" she exclaimed, eyes flashing.

They began walking slowly back along the path they had taken but had taken only a few steps when Ravenwilde stopped suddenly and exclaimed, "Oh, my God. Where is Miss Hampton?"

Stunned, Sarah began to retrace the few steps they had taken, the pain in her ankle completely forgotten. Looking down, she said, "There she is."

"Where?"

"Here, on the ground. The silly creature has fainted on us! Of all things! As if we did not have enough on our plates! Oh, do stop laughing, Ravenwilde. I haven't any smelling salts with me, or any at home either, come to that, but depend upon it, Miss Hampton will have some in her reticule if I can but find it. Ah, here it is." And with that she raised the lady's head and began waving the salts back and forth under her delicate nostrils until she was rewarded with sounds of gentle moaning.

"There now, Miss Hampton, stand up. Here, let me help you. No, no, do not go off into hysterics just now. Save it until later," Sarah admonished her. However, it was to no avail, for the lady began crying and screaming that they would all be killed and other things along the same lines.

"Now she screams," Sarah said with some asperity. "A short time ago we could have used her screams. They might have brought help, but now when they are of no use to us at all, she *will* get hysterical. Ravenwilde, *will* you stop laughing?"

In the event, however, the screams did do some good, for they brought two gentlemen who, after being apprised of what had happened, between them were very helpful in assisting Miss Hampton back to their box. Their progress was necessarily slow because of Miss Hampton's frequent attacks of weakness, which rendered her incapable of walking for some minutes, and also because of Sarah's ankle, which caused her to lean rather heavily on Ravenwilde's arm.

"I shan't waste time and breath begging your pardon for leaning so heavily upon you, your grace, for I am persuaded that you are aware of my mortification at being obliged to do so. I should rather talk more to the purpose. Who were those men and why do they wish to do you harm?"

"Your imagination is running away from you, my dear. They were no doubt simply footpads bent upon robbery. The knife was merely used as an instrument to intimidate."

"Please, Ravenwilde," Sarah responded with asperity. "You may not wish to disclose to me the truth of the matter, and I do assure you I will respect your privacy, but do not, I pray you, treat me like a ninnyhammer. I cut my eyeteeth long ago, you know. And besides, it was clear from what they said that they were expressly looking for *you* and not just someone to rob."

Stopping abruptly, Ravenwilde asked, "Do you think Miss Hampton heard what they said?"

"I do not doubt that she heard, but I seriously doubt she realized the *significance* of what she heard, for you must know, she has much more hair than wit. However, come to think on it, she might not have heard. I do not know precisely at what point she fainted, though now I think on it, it was probably when one of the assailants pushed us aside. No, she might not have heard."

"Well, let us hope she did not. I shouldn't like my

grandmother to think someone is trying to kill me. I do not want her to worry, you know."

"Indeed, no," Sarah agreed at once, "and rest assured that *I* shall say nothing to her. I am persuaded that you know more about the attack than you are willing to tell me, and I suppose you have reasons which *you*, at least, think valid, so I'll not tease you any more. However, I think that in future when I am going to be in your company, I shall carry a small pistol in my reticule."

"Do you know how to use one?" Ravenwilde asked curiously.

"Of course I do," she replied. "My father taught me years ago. The pistol I speak of is very small and no good at all at long ranges, but I do assure you that at close range, it is quite deadly."

By this time they had reached their own party, and after restoring Miss Hampton to the bosom of her mama, Ravenwilde thanked the two gentlemen for their help and assured them that further assistance would not be required. Then he set about the task of assuring Mrs. Hampton that no harm had come to Miss Hampton except for a severe assault upon her nerves. Mr. Hampton was speechless; though Mr. Leghorne too remained silent, he looked at Ravenwilde speculatively.

Meanwhile, Sarah was saying to the duchess, "Oh, ma'am. The most infamous thing! We were set upon by two footpads, one of whom attacked Ravenwilde from behind. Can you imagine anything more cowardly?"

Looking worriedly at her grandson, the duchess said, "Is he ... ?"

"Oh, no, ma'am, he came to no harm at all." Making no attempt to disguise the laughter in her voice as she watched Ravenwilde trying to reassure Mrs.

Hampton, she added, "And I am persuaded he would rather deal with a *dozen* footpads bent upon robbing him than deal with Mrs. Hampton at this moment."

Feeling that Sarah could not be so lighthearted if there had been any real danger, the duchess allowed herself to relax and enjoy the humor of the situation her grandson was in. On the one hand, Mrs. Hampton did not want to offend the duke, but on the other, she felt it her duty as a mother to make known her displeasure in him for introducing her daughter to a dangerous situation.

"But I assure you, ma'am," Ravenwilde was saying, "had I had the least notion that such a thing would happen, I would not have taken the ladies down the path. I regret the lady's nerves have been overset, but no real harm has been done."

When Miss Hampton was quieted sufficiently, the party made its way back to the carriages. It was agreed that it would be better for Miss Hampton to return home in the company of her mama. It was not until they had seen the Hampton carriage off that the duchess noticed that Sarah was limping. "My dear," she exclaimed, "you are hurt."

"Only slightly, I assure you, ma'am. Nothing to signify. I have only bruised my ankle a little. I am sure it will be all right tomorrow."

When Ravenwilde was able, he drew Sarah aside and said, "Thank you again, my dear, for handling my grandmother so well."

"Nonsense, sir. I do not know what you are talking about."

"Don't try to fool me, my girl. While *most* of my attention was engaged in soothing Mrs. and Miss Hampton, I nonetheless heard what you said to her, and more important, the *way* you said it. She has no idea the incident was more than a simple attempt to rob me."

"Then you do admit there was more to it than that, don't you?"

"Well, perhaps," he replied reluctantly, "but I am not prepared to talk about it just now. You do understand, don't you?"

"Of course, and I promise I shan't nag. But you will take care, won't you? They might make another attempt," she begged, looking into his face with her clear gray eyes.

"Oh, yes, you may rest assured that I shall take every precaution. You might find it hard to understand, but I have grown rather fond of this thick hide of mine over the years."

"Oh, indeed," she replied with a twinkle. "It passes all understanding."

"Vixen."

"Come, Harry," the Duchess of Bloomington called. "We must not keep Sarah standing. Remember her ankle."

"Forgive me, Sarah," Ravenwilde begged. "I had forgotten that you hurt your ankle. And what is worse, you hurt it in my defense."

"A mere nothing, believe me," she replied.

It was not until she was alone in her room reflecting upon the events of the evening that it struck her how very close Ravenwilde had come to being killed and she began to tremble.

Sarah limped into the breakfast room the next morning just as her aunt was finishing her own meal. With shock and concern, Mrs. Mashburne rushed to her side to help her to the table. "My dear," she exclaimed, "what in the world happened to you?"

After settling herself at the table and allowing her aunt to serve her, Sarah gave Mrs. Mashburne an expurgated version of the previous night's events, making light of the attempt on Ravenwilde's life and her own part in the drama. Basically she told Mrs. Mashburne the same story she had told the duchess, and in spite of her concern, Mrs. Mashburne was able to laugh with Sarah over the duke's discomfiture when he had to face the formidable Mrs. Hampton and explain how it came about that he was returning her daughter to her in a state of hysterical collapse.

"You can depend upon it, dear Aunt Silvia, we shan't see much of Miss Hampton for at least a week. Even if she were inclined to go about in public, her mama would never consent to it. We will be hearing everywhere how Miss Hampton's nerves have been completely shattered and how, upon the advice of their physician, she is forced to remain quietly at home to restore herself."

Although she smiled, Mrs. Mashburne said, "Well, my dear, I should think that an experience such as that *would* quite overset one so young. You must remember that we are not all as strong as you."

Flushing slightly at the mild rebuke, Sarah answered, "Indeed, yes, and I did not mean to make light of the young lady's ordeal. In point of fact, I rather like the child. She is somewhat shy and something of a peagoose, but prettily behaved and anxious to please. I have a feeling that her mama is promoting the match with Ravenwilde, and more than that, that the girl's affections are already engaged elsewhere. Even though Ravenwilde professes not to believe in love, I cannot believe he would pursue his present course with Miss Hampton if he were aware of her feelings for another."

Watching her niece closely, Mrs. Mashburne asked, "Do you intend to tell him?"

"I? Oh, no! After all, it is no bread and butter of mine," Sarah answered perhaps a little too casually.

"No, of course not," the older lady answered while avoiding Sarah's eyes by pouring each of them a fresh cup of coffee.

The ladies had barely settled themselves in the small Yellow Saloon, Mrs. Mashburne with a book and Sarah holding Casper on her lap, when Lady Ainsberry was announced. After the women had greeted one another fondly, Lady Ainsberry said, "You must forgive me for calling so early, but when I learned of last night's adventure and of your injury, dear Sarah, I felt I must call upon you to ease my mind. You are quite sure you are all right?"

"Oh, yes, quite sure," Sarah answered with a convincing smile. "I assure you my physical injury is nothing more than a bruised ankle, not even a sprain, really, and as my aunt has just recently reminded me, I am totally lacking in delicacy and so my nerves have not been affected at all."

Turning to Lady Ainsberry, Mrs. Mashburne said laughingly, "I assure you, my lady, that I said no such thing. I merely pointed out to Sarah that all ladies are not as strong as she. I should think it wonderful, indeed, if one so young as Miss Hampton were *not* adversely affected by last night's events, and I cannot see her as an object of ridicule for fainting."

"No, nor can I," Sarah answered with an irrepressible gurgle of laughter. "To own the truth, far from laughing at her, I was very much vexed when I found that she had fainted, and when I finally brought her around, what must she do but go off into strong hysterics. At that time, I found nothing to laugh about, for you must know I was most anxious for us to rejoin our party lest those wretched men decided to return. But tell me, Margaret, how came you to learn about our little adventure so early in the morning? I know news travels fast in London, but this is a little too fast, even for the ton."

"Oliver and Ravenwilde were engaged today to attend a race and were to leave quite early. Ravenwilde came by to tell Oliver that he would not be able to leave until somewhat later than planned because, due to last night's events, he would be obliged to call upon Miss Hampton this morning to inquire about her health. They decided to leave around noon and stay over for tomorrow's races as well."

For reasons Sarah could not explain, she felt a queer disappointment upon hearing that Ravenwilde would be away for two days and at least one night and possibly two, and as if talking about him somehow conjured up the gentleman, Stevens, at that very moment, announced the Duke of Ravenwilde. Paying no attention to the other two ladies in the room, he made his way straight to Sarah and, possessing himself of one of her hands, said warmly, "Ah, my dear Sarah, I see you are in your usual good looks this morning, but tell me truthfully, how are you *really?* Does your ankle give you much pain? Have you summoned the doctor yet? Here," he said, dropping to one knee, "let me take a look at it."

In shocked tones but with a twinkle in her eyes, Sarah quickly removed her foot from his reach and said, "Indeed I will not, sir. I do assure you my injury is of the slightest. I have had far worse injuries than this, and as you can see, I survived."

Once again poor Casper was dumped onto the floor because of a sudden start from his mistress. His injured eyes clearly showed he knew Ravenwilde to be the cause of yet another ignoble fall, but having learned his lesson well, he merely remained where he had fallen and watched his grace worriedly. Both Sarah and Ravenwilde laughed, each remembering another time and another place.

At last taking note of the other two ladies, the duke sprang to his feet and said, "I do beg your pardons, ladies, but you must know that Sarah's injury occurred when she came to my aid, and I was anxious to reasure myself that she sustained no serious wound. I do believe and do not hesitate to tell you that I owe my life to her."

"Nonsense, Ravenwilde. You make too much of a feeble effort. Now had I been a man—"

Mrs. Mashburne interrupted Sarah to ask if his grace would care for some refreshments, thereby denying him as well as Lady Ainsberry the pleasure of hearing just what Sarah would have done had she been a man. Lady Ainsberry was seen to approve of her action, but the expression on the duke's face clearly showed that he was very much interested to learn what Sarah was about to reveal, and the private look he exchanged with her clearly indicated his disappointment. Laughing, Sarah said, "Ravenwilde, you are a wretch."

Seeing on what easy terms Sarah and Ravenwilde were, Lady Ainsberry and Mrs. Mashburne exchanged their own significant looks.

Refusing the proffered refreshments, Ravenwilde explained that he and Lord Ainsberry were off to the races. While he spoke, the duke gently scratched behind Casper's ears, causing him to shiver with pleasure. He then admonished the pup to take care of his mistress in his absence. Abandoning Casper, the duke turned back to Sarah and begged her to take care of herself while he was away.

"Oh, I shall be perfectly all right with *Casper* to guard me. He would not dare let anything happen to me after *you* admonished him to take care." Abandoning her lighthearted banter, she stretched out one hand (which Ravenwilde clasped between both of his) and said softly, "You will be careful, won't you?"

Carrying her hand to his lips, Ravenwilde gently kissed it and said softly while looking at her in a way that caused her heart to do flips, "Of course, my dear. You musn't worry about me. I have been in much tighter spots than this, you know."

"No," she answered, raising one delicate eyebrow, "I did not know."

Realizing that once again he had said more than he ought, the duke laughed and said, "But of course. How could I not have been, having traveled as widely as I have? Every country is not as civilized as England, you know."

"Indeed?" Sarah answered skeptically.

Once again possessing himself of Sarah's hands, he gave them a gentle squeeze before taking leave of the ladies, and while Mrs. Mashburne and Lady Ainsberry again exchanged meaningful glances, Sarah sat for some few minutes looking at the door through which Ravenwilde's broad back had disappeared.

After several days, Sarah's ankle felt well enough for her to venture into society again. She had received a note from Ravenwilde inquiring about her health and informing her that he would be away longer than first expected. He and Lord Ainsberry had received intelligence about a mill which was to be fought in the immediate neighborhood a day or two hence, and since they were already there, it would be a shame not to stay and enjoy the entertainment. Of course, there was no sense in returning to London and then making another journey back.

Sarah could not feel easy about these arrangements, for she had a fair idea of the types of people who attended these functions. Not only the gentlemen of the ton were addicted to such events, but much of the riffraff were also. She consoled herself with the knowledge that at least he was not alone and thought wryly that Lord Ainsberry would be far better able to lend assistance than she had been should the need again arise.

Upon her arrival at a ball given by one of her mother's friends, a lady whom Sarah remembered with affection because of various kindnesses bestowed upon her during childhood, she was surprised to see Miss Hampton and Mr. Leghorne in conversation across the room and immediately made her way to them. "Miss Hampton," she said warmly, "how glad I am to see you out and about so soon. I feared you would not be among us for some days yet. How are you?"

Even though the younger lady was looking rather pale and wan, she answered with a sweet smile, "Mama wanted me to stay at home for a few more days, but I persuaded her that my cousin could take care of me and would return me home should I feel the least bit tired." The two exchanged such a look of devotion that Sarah was convinced of her suspicion that they had formed a previous attachment.

"Please take my chair, Miss Windemere," Mr. Leghorne said. "I was just about to procure refreshments for Alethia. May I bring you something?"

"Yes, thank you, Mr. Leghorne. That would be lovely. To own the truth, I still sometimes feel a slight twinge in my ankle and I should be glad to rest for a few minutes."

Sarah watched Miss Hampton's face as her cousin walked away from them. Suddenly the younger lady's face seemed to crumple, and Sarah had an uneasy feeling that she was about to be subjected to yet another fit of the vapors, but Miss Hampton controlled herself with a truly valiant effort. However, she turned to Sarah and said tearfully, "Oh, Miss Windemere, I do not know what I shall do. Mama is determined that I shall marry Ravenwilde, and until Ivan returned I was content to go along with her wishes. However, now that he is back, I know that I am still in love with him and he with me. You see, we grew up together and have been very close since we were children, even though he is older than I. When he joined the army, I begged him to take me with him, but he said I was too young to know my mind and heart and that if I still felt the same way when the war was over, we would see what could be done. He urged me to go along as if there were nothing between us, to meet other men and enjoy my come-out, and for a while, with all the excitement of the season and everything, I thought what I had felt for him was mere infatuation. There was, nevertheless, something that kept me from accepting any of the offers I received during my first season, but this year Ravenwilde came along and Mama told me I owed it to the family to encourage him. At first it was very flattering to have the Duke of Ravenwilde pay attention to me, but now I see that I mean nothing to him. He is merely looking for a marriage of convenience and has settled upon me as someone young and healthy enough and with the right background to be the mother of his heir. Indeed, ma'am," she continued guilelessly, "I think he is much fonder of *you* than of me, and if you were not so *old*, he would be paying his addresses to you."

Sarah managed to turn a choking sound into a cough as Miss Hampton finished her artless observations. She wished with all her heart that Raven-wilde might hear the child's utterances. The thought of the unholy amusement which would dance in his brown eyes almost overset her gravity, for she doubted not for a moment that his amusement would be as great as her own. Controlling herself admirably, she was able to say, "But, my dear, if you truly feel a lasting tendre for your cousin, surely your mama will not try to force you into marriage with someone else."

"Oh, perhaps not with just *anyone* else," Miss Hampton answered, "but the Duke of Ravenwilde is not just *anyone*. Mama says that in spite of his reputation, he seems to have settled down some now and even if he should seek pleasure outside of marriage, well, that does not signify, because most gentlemen keep a mistress tucked away and that I shouldn't let it bother me. She says the title and money will give me an enviable position in society and that when I am a duchess I shall be in a position to help my sisters make suitable matches. She says just think what consequence I shall enjoy by being in some way related to the Duchess of Bloomington, but to own the truth, ma'am, that lady terrifies me."

Although Sarah was very much taken aback by these artless confessions, she was nonetheless wryly amused when she reflected on what would be Mrs. Hampton's reaction if she knew what secrets her innocent daughter was revealing. "But surely your mama cannot *force* you to accept an offer from Ravenwilde. Simply explain to her that you have already formed a tendre for someone else."

Even Sarah realized the inappropriateness of this advice, for she knew that Miss Hampton's character was not of the strongest and that her resolve, or the strength to carry it through, was nonexistent. Even now she thought she saw a look bordering on terror in the younger girl's eyes as she said, "Oh, I couldn't possibly do that. You do not know how angry Mama can become when one crosses her."

"Well, if you cannot or will not stand up to her," Sarah answered with asperity, "I do not see that you have any choice but to marry whomever your mama directs you to marry."

Miss Hampton turned pleading, tear-filled eyes to Sarah and begged, "Could you not tell the duke of my plight, ma'am? I know that he holds you in affection and will listen to you. If he should cry off, Mama could not blame me and Ivan and will perhaps consent to our engagement. She has said that I *must* be settled this season, for she has to bring out my sister next year. It isn't as if he has already declared himself. Please, Miss Windemere, could you not talk to Ravenwilde for me? Perhaps a word from you would prevent him from speaking to Papa."

"Indeed no!" Sarah answered, shocked but a little amused also. "It would be the greatest impertinence on earth should I attempt to interfere in his grace's affairs. I do assure you, Miss Hampton, as much as I sympathize with your plight, my friendship with Ravenwilde is not such that I would feel comfortable in doing as you ask. No, I am sorry, but that is out of the question."

When Mr. Leghorne returned and saw the obvious distress on Miss Hampton's face, he said, "You must excuse us, Miss Windemere. It appears Mrs. Hampton was right. I shall take Miss Hampton home immediately."

Miss Windemere said all that was proper and watched as Mr. Leghorne solicitously led Miss Hampton from the room. She pondered on the things Miss Hampton had told her but could see nothing she herself could do about the girl's dilemma. The best thing for Miss Hampton to do, of course, was to tell her mama that she had no intentions of marrying anyone except her cousin and then stick to her resolve. However, Sarah was enough of a realist to know that such a course of action was easier planned than followed, and for one with Miss Hampton's disposition, almost impossible. She knew that if her father had not left her independently wealthy, she would have had a much harder time than she had had resisting Judith's pressures upon her to take a husband, but she had no doubts at all that she *would* have successfully resisted.

She was truly sorry for Miss Hampton, but had to admit to herself that it was for Ravenwilde that she felt the most. He deserved more than a wife who was marrying him solely because her ambitious mama was forcing her to. But would it really matter to him? After all, he had said that love meant nothing to him. Perhaps he would actually prefer a wife who felt nothing at all for him, since he himself felt nothing.

Using her ankle as an excuse, Sarah returned home early that evening and spent a restless night. She awoke with a blinding headache, but after eating a substantial breakfast and drinking two cups of coffee, she was able to relate to Mrs. Mashburne her conversation with Miss Hampton with a great deal of her natural humor.

"Can you imagine, Aunt Silvia, Mrs. Hampton's chagrin if she knew the things Miss Hampton revealed to me? That lady would be absolutely livid," she said laughingly.

"Indeed, and who could blame her?" Mrs. Mashburne answered. "I have always thought girls were thrown into society much too young. They have no experience in society and have no idea about how to go on. Of course, the girl has been out for two years now, but still, she is just a baby. Poor little thing, being forced into a marriage with a man like Ravenwilde!"

"A man like Ravenwilde?" Sarah asked more sharply than she realized. "What, I pray, is wrong with Ravenwilde? His manners are perhaps a little too informal for some, but I never took *you* to be one of those boring sticklers."

Very much surprised and taken aback, for Sarah had never spoken so sharply to her before, Mrs. Mashburne protested, "Really, my love, I meant to cast no aspersions on the gentleman's character. I merely meant that he is much older than she, not only in actual years but in experience as well. He is, as you must admit, a man of the world, knowledgeable and sophisticated, while she is still a child."

"Forgive me, dear Aunt," Sarah said, reaching across the table to clasp her aunt's hand. "I have a wretched headache. Perhaps Miss Hampton is right; I am getting old—too old, at any rate, for the rigors of a London season. I think I shall write to Foxborough today and inform the servants that I shall return home next week."

Unaccountably, her lovely gray eyes had filled with tears. Seeing this, Mrs. Mashburne rushed to her side and, taking her into her arms as one would embrace a small child, she said, "Nonsense, my love. You are just tired. The experience at Vauxhall Gardens no doubt affected you more than you knew, and say what you will, I am persuaded that your ankle is still bothering you."

"I am sorry," Sarah said, recovering quickly. "You are right, of course, my ankle *does* still bother me. I think I shall stay close for a few more days. There is nothing going forward right now that interests me anyway. I shall send around a note to Lady Grossener crying off from her picnic this afternoon. I am sure she will understand. I haven't accepted anything else this week except an invitation to a rout at Lady Gresham's on Friday. I will wait a day or two to see how I feel before crying off from that."

Privately Mrs. Mashburne thought there was more bothering Sarah than her ankle and felt she needed something to divert her mind, so she said, "I think that is wise, love, but if you feel up to it tomorrow, I would appreciate it very much if you would go shopping with me for about an hour. There are a few things I need to refurbish my wardrobe, and no one has your eye for color and match. If you do not feel up to it, pray tell me and we can perhaps go another day."

"I should love to go," Sarah assured her. "It will be fun as well as diverting. We haven't been shopping since we first came to London."

Laughingly, Mrs. Mashburne answered, "We haven't *needed* to shop after *those* extravagant trips. I still feel guilty when I remember all the things I let you buy for me."

"Do not be foolish, dear Aunt. You know it was not that much, and besides, I can never repay you for all your kindness."

"Now who is being foolish?" her aunt replied, misty-eyed.

When the ladies parted for an afternoon rest, Mrs. Mashburne reflected on Sarah's unusual behavior and sadly came to the conclusion that the girl had fallen in love. She was not aware of it as yet, but so it was.

Chapter 8

As luck would have it, just as they stepped from their carriage on Bond Street, Ravenwilde's cousin, Donnelly, was strolling down the street, and there was nothing for it but for Sarah to introduce him to her aunt.

"I see beauty is a family trait," Donnelly said with a smooth voice and an accompanying practiced smile which made the hair on Sarah's arms stand on end. What was it about the man that suggested something sinister? Giving herself a mental shake, she was about to take leave of him when he reached out and touched her arm.

"Please stay a moment, Miss Windemere. I have not seen my cousin for several days. Perhaps you can tell me, is he out of town?"

Looking pointedly at his hand on her arm, Sarah moved away from him and said in wintry tones, "I really cannot say, sir. Perhaps if you called at his home?"

"Yes, of course, I could do that," he answered smoothly, "but I had heard that he had traveled out of town for some sort of race or mill. If he has not returned, there is no reason for me to call at his home. I merely thought you could save me an unnecessary trip," he said with what Sarah was sure he considered to be a disarming smile.

"Yes, well, I am afraid I cannot help you," she replied. "You really must excuse us. My aunt and I have some shopping to do before returning home."

"Of course," he answered, bowing slightly. "Your servant, ladies."

"What a dreadful man!" Mrs. Mashburne exclaimed. "The nerve of him, asking you about Ravenwilde's movements just as if you lived in his pocket. I never heard of such impertinence."

"Yes," Sarah agreed, "he is quite the most odious man I have ever met. One wonders how Ravenwilde and he can be from the same family, however remotely related they may be. I cannot like the man, Aunt Silvia, and the more I see of him, the more inclined I am to agree with the duchess. She thinks him evil. But come, let us get on with our shopping."

When they reached home, Stevens told them that Lady Ainsberry was waiting for them in the Blue Saloon. Without taking time to remove her hat and pelisse, Sarah went directly to her after instructing Stevens to bring refreshments immediately.

The bright smile of greeting froze on Sarah's face when she saw the stricken look Lady Ainsberry cast her when she opened the door. "Margaret, my dear, what is amiss? Is it Oliver? Has he had an accident?

133

Come, sit by the fire. Stevens will bring tea in a moment."

"Oh, Sarah," she cried, "It isn't Oliver—It is Ravenwilde. He has been shot!"

Clutching her hands to her sides, Sarah felt all the blood drain from her face. For a moment she was too horrified to speak. With a great effort she finally managed to whisper, "Is he dead?"

"Oh, no, my dear. Not dead, nor anywhere near it. Oliver assures me in the letter he sent—here, read for yourself—that it is only a flesh wound and that Ravenwilde would have ridden back to London immediately. However, since he had lost some blood, Oliver thought it safer for them to stay at the inn overnight and hire a carriage to bring them back tomorrow. Sarah, are you all right?"

Before Sarah answered, Mrs. Mashburne entered the room, and, seeing Sarah's pale face and stricken eyes, she rushed to her and leading her to the sofa in front of the fire, gently settled her among the soft cushions. "Please ring for Stevens, Lady Ainsberry, and request some brandy." Since Sarah seemed incapable of telling her what was wrong, she turned to Lady Ainsberry for enlightenment when Stevens had brought the brandy and left the room.

While Sarah obediently sipped from the snifter Mrs. Mashburn handed her, Lady Ainsberry explained what what happened. "But everything is all right, Sarah. No real harm was done," Mrs. Mashburne tried to reassure her.

"No, not this time, nor the last. But what about the next time, Aunt Silvia?" Sarah answered dully.

Worriedly her aunt suggested, "Please, my little love, I think you should go to bed for a while. I am sure Lady Ainsberry will excuse you, won't you, my lady?"

"No, no, I am all right now," Sarah replied, and indeed the color was returning to her face and she seemed to be regaining control over herself. "How foolish of me, but I do assure you, I am perfectly all right now. Tell me, Margaret, did Oliver tell you anything else?"

She apparently had forgotten that she was holding the letter Lord Ainsberry had sent to his wife, and Margaret, exchanging glances with Mrs. Mashburne, saw no reason to remind her. "Not much, my dear. Only that they were riding back to their inn after seeing the mill when they were ambushed. The assailant apparently was concealed behind some rocks on a hillside. Fortunately, Ravenwilde's horse shied away from some trash that was blowing across the road and the man's aim was ruined. Oliver got Ravenwilde back to the inn as quickly as possible and called a doctor. The shot merely grazed his arm, but was deep enough to cause some little bleeding. Apparently he will be able to travel tomorrow, and we should see him in London before nightfall."

"I must go to him," Sarah said steadily, "just as soon as he arrives home."

"Oh, no, my dear," Mrs. Mashburne exclaimed, shocked. "You cannot do that! A lady *cannot* visit a gentleman's home."

"No, I suppose not," Sarah agreed reluctantly, "but I must see him as soon as possible. I shall send a note around to his home requesting him to call upon me the moment he is well enough."

"I cannot like that idea either, but I do not suppose it can do much harm," her aunt conceded with a worried look to Lady Ainsberry.

"Has anyone informed the duchess?" Sarah asked.

"No," replied Lady Ainsberry, "and Ravenwilde

specifically asked that she not be told of these events. He does not want to worry her unnecessarily."

A tender smile, which was not lost on her two companions, touched Sarah's generous mouth as she said, "No, *he* wouldn't."

Lady Ainsberry soon took leave of the ladies. Sarah was still unconciously holding Oliver's letter, and Margaret thought it best to leave it with her. Later, when she was thinking more clearly, she would discover that she had it and be somewhat reassured by its contents.

Mrs. Mashburne followed Lady Ainsberry to the door. Pulling on her gloves, Lady Ainsberry said, "She is in love with him, isn't she?"

"Yes," sighed Mrs. Mashburne," I am afraid she is. I am not sure she realizes it yet, but I have suspected for a long time, almost from the beginning, that she was forming an attachment for him. Poor darling, she has never been close to being in love before. I'm afraid she will break her heart over this." Tears were streaming down her lovely face, but she was totally unaware of them. "I had so hoped that she would someday meet the right man, but I know she will never marry. A girl like Sarah loves only once. Oh, why did I leave it to Ravenwilde?"

"You really must not let her see you like this, Mrs. Mashburne," Lady Ainsberry chided gently. "I know it is hard for you, but believe me, Ravenwilde is not such a bad man. In fact, I think he and Sarah would make a good match. Do not look so surprised, my dear. He has never been in love either, you know."

"But what about Miss Hampton?" Mrs. Mashburne asked.

"I cannot believe such a man as Ravenwilde would willingly tie himself to such a peagoose as Miss

Hampton. He would be ready to strangle her within a fortnight. Not that she is not a lovely, biddable girl, but I cannot believe he likes simpletons, no matter how biddable they may be."

Feeling much better, Mrs. Mashburne went back to Sarah and found her reading Lord Ainsberry's letter.

Sarah was alone when Stevens announced Ravenwilde three days later. It had been a damp and dreary day, and Sarah had spent most of the morning gazing out the window at the gray sky. When Ravenwilde entered the room it seemed to her that the sun had suddenly appeared and lit up the whole world.

Advancing toward him with outstretched hands, she said, "Ravenwilde, you *are* all right, aren't you?"

"Yes, of course," he answered with a smile. "I am not that easy to kill, you know.

Sarah's lovely brow was furrowed with worry lines as she looked into his face and asked, "But who is it who wants you dead, and why?"

Leading her to the sofa, he settled himself at her side, apparently unaware that he was still holding her hand. "I do not know, and that is what makes the whole thing so difficult. Always before I have been able to identify the enemy. Survival is so much easier, my dear, if one knows who is the enemy."

Reluctantly freeing her hand from his, Sarah said, "You have alluded to past dangers before, Ravenwilde, can you not tell me about it?"

Searching her face intently, he answered, "Yes, I suppose I can and should." He stood up and walked over to the fireplace, where he leaned one arm on the mantel. "My grandmother is the only other person, outside the government officials who were also involved in some way, who knows what I was doing these past years. What I am about to tell you is confidential, and I know I need not ask you to keep it to yourself. I do not think there is any danger to me from my past actions, but most of what I did was strictly unofficial—that is to say, not *officially* sanctioned by our government. However, in times of war or threats of war, many necessary things are done *unofficially*," he said wryly.

"As you know, my father remarried some months before I left England. He was besotted with the lady. I do not think he was ever really in love with my mother. Of course, he felt a fondness for her but he had fallen completely in love with my stepmother, and oh, God, what a fool she played him for!" A note of anguished fury had entered his voice and his eyes were as cold as steel as he continued. "I swore at that time I would never love a woman enough to let her do to me what she did to my father, but just lately," he continued, his voice softening, "I have begun to think...But never mind the fact is that she destroyed him! Oh, yes, the gossips say *I* was the cause of his death, but that is not true. When he discovered her perfidy, he lost all will to live, My father was a proud man and to know he had been cuckolded, not once, but many times, was more than he could bear.

"A week before I left England, my stepmother sent word to me that she and my father wanted to see me in her bedchamber. I should have suspected a trap, but I did not. I already knew I was going to be away for quite some time, and I took every opportunity to be with my father those last few days. When I entered her room, there was no one there except my stepmother. She told me that my father would be along shortly and offered me a drink. It soon became apparent to me what she had in mind, and as I was leaving she threw herself upon my chest. While I was trying to disengage her arms from around my neck, my father walked in. I shall never forget the look of horror on his face when he saw his wife and son in an apparent embrace. Of course, she told him that it was I who had come to her room uninvited and attempted to seduce her. My father said not a word, but merely turned and, with the greatest dignity I have ever seen in a man's bearing, walked slowly back to his own rooms. I followed him and attempted to explain without speaking too harshly about his wife. He interrupted my explanations and told me that he had been aware for quite some time that his wife was unfaithful, but that he had never dreamed she would try anything with his son.

"We had a long talk that night, lasting until dawn began to break. I told him that I had been approached by an old school friend who was currently working with our Foreign Office, and who wanted to recruit me for a very delicate secret mission and that I had accepted. We were not at war with France at that time, but it was obvious to anyone who cared to read the signs that it would not be long. Our Foreign Office felt it was necessary to position men in various foreign countries, including France, to establish contacts and create a network of spies who could furnish us information when war did break out. My immediate job was to set up such a network in France, particularly along the coast. I was to travel incognito, indeed to try to pass myself off as a Frenchman. My command of the language is very good, and with my coloring, that part of the task was not too difficult. I told my father all this and pledged him to secrecy. We concocted a story which would explain my absence from England, but in the event, our story was not necessary. As you know, my stepmother told her own story, and it was assumed my father drove me away. He was a man of great perception and intelligence who had an enormous sense of country and honor. He made me promise before I left that I would not return home until the job was done, no matter what happened. That is why I did not return when he died. I knew he would not want me to. All my correspondence to him while he lived, to my grandmother, and to my bailiff were routed by the Foreign Office to India and back to England. I did not actually go to India until after the war, and I only stayed a few months. When the war actually began, my work was pretty much finished in France and I was used as a courier between our generals and as a spy behind enemy lines. I had turned over the spy network to those whom I knew I could trust. At the end, I was with Wellington."

For the first time Sarah interrupted and said with some horror, "You were at Waterloo?"

He smiled wryly and answered, "Yes, in a manner of speaking. Actually, you know, the battle was not really fought at Waterloo. It was fought some seven miles away at La Belle-Alliance. Our troops were ranged along a ridge at the town of Mont-Saint-Jean, and four miles to the south were Napolean's forces on a ridge facing La Belle-Alliance. It had been raining," Ravenwilde continued with a bleak, faraway look in his eyes that told Sarah he was reliving all the horror of that final battle. "Between the two ridges was a valley—a valley of death. For over eight hours, thousands of Englishmen and Frenchmen fought and died in that valley. The mud was soaked with blood, and at the end, more than one-third of Napolean's men were wounded or dead. It was said of Napoleon, and I believe it, that he wept and wished that he, too, had died."

"Oh, Ravenwilde," Sarah cried, rising from her seat and going to him. She touched his arm in an effort to bring him back from the horrors of the battlefield. "How awful for you."

"Not as awful for me as for some," he answered bleakly. "I survived; many did not."

As horrible as the prospect of someone trying to kill him now might be, Sarah felt it would be better for him to think upon that than to dwell upon the agony of the war. In an effort to divert his mind from that she asked, "Are you sure no one from your past—I mean, during your activities before the war—could have hunted you down for revenge? They do say hatred dies hard for a defeated people."

"I am not *absolutely* sure, of course, but I do not think so. I think the culprit is much closer to home," he answered.

"But you will be careful, won't you?" she asked worriedly.

Smiling at her, he answered, "You may be sure of it, and I wish you will not worry. I think that whoever it is is becoming desperate, and desperate men always make mistakes. He has failed at ambush, so he must come out more into the open. When he does that, I will be prepared."

Sarah wished that she could feel just a little of the confidence Ravenwilde apparently felt, and she told him so.

He merely laughed and promised to see her at Lady Gresham's ball that evening. When he had taken his leave of her, Sarah sat pondering the incredible story he had told her. She had never once believed him capable of doing anything dishonorable, but never in her wildest dreams would she have imagined the truth about his long absence from England.

When Sarah, accompanied by Mrs. Mashburne and Mr. Brooks arrived at Lady Gresham's ball, her eyes automatically scanned the room for Ravenwilde. She was somewhat disappointed that she could not find him but consoled herself with the knowledge that he had told her he would be there and allowed herself to be led in a country dance by one of the numerous young men who considered it a mark of his maturity to be seen dancing with the dashing and beautiful Miss Windemere.

At the end of the dance the young gentleman properly led her back to her aunt, where she engaged in somewhat distracted conversation while all the time searching the sea of faces for Ravenwilde. She was becoming a little worried. What if he had been attacked again? What if he was even now lying mortally wounded? Stop it! she told herself. There could be dozens of reasons for his lateness, and even if he did not show up at all, it did not mean anything was seriously amiss. After all, he had been wounded recently. It would not be wonderful if he simply did not feel like going to a ball tonight.

So great was her relief when she finally spotted him that she instinctively made a move toward where he was standing surveying the crowded room. Mrs. Mashburne laid a restraining hand on her arm and said softly, "No, my love, you must not. There are those watching you who would be delighted to see you make such an improper move. Not everyone agrees with your decision to set up your own establishment, and taking note of your friendship with Ravenwilde, some tattlemongers have even gone so far as to make dire predictions as to the outcome of your actions." When Sarah, with eyes flashing, opened her mouth to protest, Mrs. Mashburne continued, "Shush, now, child. I know what you will say, but think for a moment. You *cannot* want to tie your garter in public."

Realizing the truth of her aunt's words, Sarah smiled and said, "Thank you, dear Aunt. You are right, of course. I fear I am a great trial to you."

"Nonsense. We all of us forget ourselves occasionally. It is only that just now, it would be particularly harmful to you to make a slip. The smallest indiscretion would be blown all out of proportion. And besides, your impulsive gesture was not necessary. Ravenwilde is making his way toward us now."

With a supreme effort, of which her aunt showed her approval by a slight smile, Sarah managed not to turn around to mark his progress, but continued in conversation with her aunt. Any onlooker would have supposed that she was either not aware of or indifferent to Ravenwilde's approach, but in fact, her pulses had quickened, her hands had tightened around the fan she carried, and a faint flush had crept into her face. However, she managed to greet him with at least outward composure and refrained from mentioning the lateness of his arrival until he was twirling her expertly around the dance floor to the rhythm of a waltz.

"I had begun to worry," she said. "I trust you have suffered no mishap?"

"Oh, Lord, no," he answered, "although I would almost as soon have. I was summoned to my grandmother's house. It seems someone told her about my little adventure and she was worried. I cannot imagine," he continued with a twinkle in his brown eyes, "how she manages to know everything that happens when she seldom leaves the house."

Sarah laughed and exclaimed, "Oh, Ravenwilde,

what a simpleton you are about some things. Not only *her* servants, but almost every servant in London is part of a vast network of information and gossip. They are not organized, of course, but I daresay they all know far more about what goes on in the ton than most of the members themselves. They meet and talk in pubs, at the market, in kitchens, and oh, any number of places. If my maid accompanies me on a morning call, she spends time with the maid of my friend and they exchange information. Since your grandmother seldom leaves the house, I have no doubt she has trained her servants to be particularly adept at picking up stray information. Depend upon it, someone from your household let slip the information that you had suffered an injury to someone close to her household. She probably was aware of it the day you arrived home."

Ravenwilde was so struck by what Sarah told him that he almost missed a step, thus sending Sarah into peals of laughter.

"Good God," he exclaimed. "I should have known, for I used servants extensively when I was gathering information in France. I suppose I thought things like that happened only during times of war, or that our English servants were different from those in France; more circumspect, I suppose."

"I do not think any of their gossip, or at least very little of it, is malicious," Sarah assured him. "Mostly it starts with bragging. Your servant, for example, probably commented, with a great deal of false casualness, that his master was already on his feet after suffering a grievous wound. He wanted to get across to someone else's servant that *his* master was vastly superior to the master of his friend."

Now it was Ravenwilde's turn to laugh, and not

a few heads turned to watch them twirling around the room and wondered what could be the source of the pleasure they were obviously enjoying in each other's company.

Although Ravenwilde danced with several young (and some not so young) ladies, including Miss Hampton, during the course of the evening, he returned to claim Sarah's company for supper. They shared a table with Mrs. Mashburne and Mr. Brooks, and the gossips were denied the pleasure of accusing them of trying to be alone. Sarah, as well as her aunt, was aware that she was being watched closely that evening, and far from being annoyed, she began to enjoy the situation, relishing the thoughts of the watchers' disappointment when she failed to give them anything over which to click their tongues.

She was aware that ever since the incident at Vauxhall Gardens her association with Ravenwilde had been noted. It was generally agreed among the ton, thanks mostly to Mrs. Hampton's smug assumption that Ravenwilde was seriously interested in her daughter, that an announcement would be made any day to the effect that Miss Hampton was to marry the duke. Therefore, the ton assumed that he was merely flirting with Sarah, and some said he very likely would give her a slip of the shoulder if she was not careful. This prospect was so patently absurd that Sarah smiled to think on it.

"You smile, my dear. What private thoughts do you find so amusing?" Ravenwilde asked.

"Oh, nothing much," she answered. "You must have noticed how closely we are being watched tonight. All the wags in London must be in attendance, and they are waiting for me to do something about which they can gossip. I have often thought what a pity it is that someone cannot split their tongues down the middle and tie them behind their backs. I assure you, they are quite long enough." As Ravenwilde began to choke on laughter, Sarah continued thoughtfully, "However, I do not suppose that would signify, because I am persuaded they could still talk, for their tongues are loose at *both* ends."

By this time, Ravenwilde had completely succumbed to a fit of laughter, and Sarah said, "Wretched man! Now see what you have led me to say."

"I?" Ravenwilde asked, still laughing. "I said nothing that would lead you to say what you did."

"Well, perhaps you did not," Sarah conceded. "But you must know that I would never so far forget myself as to say such things to anyone else. There is something about you which encourages me to say the most outrageous things. Heretofore, I have been content merely to *think* such things, but if you are with me, I have developed the most appalling habit of blurting out whatever comes to mind. You, sir, are a bad influence." The twinkle in her gray eyes robbed her words of any sting.

"But my dear Sarah," he answered gravely, "you know that *old* ladies are forgiven their sharp tongues."

"Odious, odious creature," she answered with a gurgle. "I shall get even with you for that."

"I tremble, for I have no doubt you will," he answered. "Then it will be bellows to mend with me."

"And I have no doubt you will quickly come around," she answered with a smile. "I shouldn't think one could give you a sharp enough setdown to flatten you for long."

"Probably not," he agreed, "for you know me to be a most ramshackle fellow."

"I know you to be the greatest fraud in nature," she answered with a fulminating glance. "Don't try

146

to throw dust in *my* eyes, sir. I am more than seven, you know."

"A facer," he answered tragically as the party rose and prepared to go back to the ballroom.

"The next waltz is mine," he reminded her as they parted, thus giving her no chance to refuse, even if she had wanted to, which she did not.

Sarah could not remember when she had enjoyed an evening more. Her ankle was completely well; she felt not a twinge as she waltzed around the room with Ravenwilde. It was easy to lose herself in the pleasure of the moment, and she was still glowing happily when she noticed Lady Waxton motioning to her.

Even though Sarah knew Lady Waxton for an inveterate gossip who tried to hide her malice by convincing the recipient of her confidences that she had someone's best interest at heart, she saw no way to avoid her but was obliged to greet the lady with the respectful good manners due her by virtue of age and position from one of Sarah's age.

"I could not help but notice, dear Sarah, that you have twice danced the waltz with Ravenwilde. It would seem that after paying very particular attentions to Miss Hampton, thus subjecting her to a great deal of comment, he is now ready to abandon her to the gossips and engage in a flirtation with *you*. Just look at the poor child. She looks as if she were being led to the guillotine rather than a country dance with her cousin."

And indeed Miss Hampton's appearance was one of abject misery, and while Sarah knew it had nothing to do with Ravenwilde's paying attention to another lady, and that nothing would please Miss Hampton more than for him to transfer *all* his attention to someone else, she had no intention of imparting this intelligence to anyone, much less to as great a gabblemonger as Lady Waxton.

Undeterred by Sarah's lack of response, Lady Waxton continued with false sweetness and sincerity, "I shouldn't want to see you hurt, my dear, and since I am a good friend of your sister's, I feel I would be derelict in my duty did I not give you some friendly advice. You must know that Judith asked me to keep an eye on you while you are in London."

Stunned as much by the older lady's directness as by the knowledge that Judith had asked her to spy upon her (for she could not see it as anything other than spying, no matter what linen Judith and Lady Waxton chose to wrap it in), Sarah protested, "Indeed, Lady Waxton, I was not aware that Judith had asked you to watch me, nor is it necessary. I think it a great piece of impertinence on Judith's part, and so I shall tell her."

"But I very much fear it *was* necessary, dear child," Lady Waxton answered in pained accents, "especially after this night's performance. While you have admittedly seen several seasons, Lord Ravenwilde has not been in town these many years and you have not before encountered him. Actually, I think the scandal broke the season before you made your come-out, and I doubt anyone saw fit to sully your innocent ears with the story of his most reprehensible behavior. Afterward, of course, he turned tail and ran. There are those who say he went to India, and judging from the color of his skin, dreadfully dark, you know, I suppose that is true. They do say the sun is unbearable there. But the color of his complexion is not the issue, is it, my dear?" she twittered, obviously pleased with her little joke, and only a little discomfited by Sarah's lack of appreciation. "Anyway, my dear, the story is—"

"I know the story, ma'am, and I know how loath you are to repeat gossip, so we'll say no more," Sarah answered coldly.

Much astonished, the lady said, "You know the story and still you stand up with him twice? Well, I must say that is strange behavior indeed."

"Not for me, ma'am. You see, I have made it an absolute rule in my life these many years to mind my own business."

"Well, I never..." Words failed the lady and she could say no more but sat with her eyes opened almost as wide as her mouth.

Prompted by an evil genius, Sarah answered sweetly, "No, but *I* have."

She felt a light touch on her shoulder and turned to see the subject of their conversation, if such it could be called, smiling down at her.

"A waltz, Miss Windemere. May I have the honor?"

Without a moment's hesitation, Sarah answered, "Of course, your grace," and floated onto the floor oblivious to everything except her anger.

When she had calmed herself somewhat, she looked up into the concerned eyes of the duke and said, "You know it is against all the rules for a gentleman to ask a lady for a third dance, and a waltz at that!"

"A lady can always refuse."

"Well, yes," she admitted, "but I was angry and not thinking straight."

"Yes, I noticed the storm in your eyes, and I must say the heightened color in your face vastly becomes you. However, I think I have told you before that you are enchanting when you are angry."

They waltzed in silence for several minutes. Neither Sarah nor Ravenwilde was unaware of the stir this third waltz was creating among the other guests, and Ravenwilde had begun to regret his impulsive action.

"I heard the whole thing, you know," he said softly, "and I was angry. Impulsively I asked you to dance. Forgive me, my love, for putting you in a position to attract speculation and gossip."

The storm had again built in Sarah's eyes, and anger put a fine edge to her normally soft and musical voice. "Gossip, sir? Surely one of my advanced years and so obviously on the shelf can be excused for breaking a rule made for the protection of the innocent girls in their first season. Anyway, what can one expect of one so beyond the pale as to set up her own establishment and leave the protection of so worthy a sister and brother-in-law as I have had the temerity to do?"

Ravenwilde felt her body sag a little in his arms, and when she again spoke her voice held a tiny tremor. "Oh, Ravenwilde, did you hear her? Judith had the nerve to ask her to *spy* on me. Can you believe one's own sister would do something so dastardly?"

"Perhaps she meant well," he answered gently. "She may have had your well-being at heart."

"You *cannot* believe that!" Sarah answered scornfully. "Everyone knows Lady Waxton for a malicious gossip and talebearer. The lady's tongue is a lethal weapon. I would as soon have a sword pointed at my heart as her tongue turned against me."

Although there was a slight twitch at the corners

of his mouth, Ravenwilde said, "You are tired. Let me take you home."

"What? Leave, and leave the arena to the gossips? No, thank you, your grace, I will stay until the bitter end."

Chapter 9

And stay she did. She was aware that her laughter had about it a brittleness and that her tongue was a little sharper than usual, but she was determined to see it through in spite of the ache that threatened to split her head wide open.

She was also aware of the worried looks bestowed upon her by her aunt, and her heart ached at the realization that she had done something that might very well cast a reflection on the lady who was supposed to be her chaperon. Not for worlds would she hurt her beloved aunt, but hurt her she had, and for the moment she could think of no way to make it up to her.

If only Aunt Silvia would scold her! But far from scolding, the older lady held her hand from the moment they entered their carriage until they arrived home. Mrs. Mashburne thanked Mr. Brooks for his escort and said all that was proper while Sarah walked up the steps like a wraith and was swallowed up in the light of the open doorway, leaving her aunt to say goodnight to Mr. Brooks.

Mrs. Mashburne wisely left Sarah to her own thoughts that night, knowing that she would have to sort things out for herself.

Much later, lying alone in bed, unable to sleep because of the headache and the tumultuous thoughts which raced through her mind, Sarah finally asked herself the question she had been avoiding all evening. Why had she allowed herself to be put in a position to be gossiped about? Indeed, her reputation had possibly been seriously compromised by this evening's work. Not only had she danced *three* times with the same gentleman (and waltzes at that!), knowing as everyone in London knew that society allowed only two, but Lady Waxton was sure to repeat their conversation to anyone who would listen. It would have been bad enough if the ladies had been an equal age, but for one of Sarah's age to give so sharp a setdown to one of Lady Waxton's advanced years was a display of rudeness and disrespect that could not be excused by polite society. Why had she done it? True, she had been blinded by anger at Judith, but stronger than that, she had to admit, was her fierce determination to stand by Ravenwilde in the face of the unwarranted slander uttered by Lady Waxton. And what if the slander had been *warranted?* Would she still have stood by him? Yes...! her heart screamed, for nothing mattered except that he not be left to stand alone. In the darkness of the night and her own despair, Sarah was forced to admit that she had thrown discretion to the winds because she had fallen in love with Raven-wilde.

Tossing and turning in her bed, Sarah relived every moment of the lovely evening which had ended so disastrously. Her stomach did a flipflop when she remembered that Ravenwilde had called her his love, but she checked her soaring hopes quickly by reminding herself that "my love" was merely a figure of speech which many gentlemen, and ladies also for that matter, frequently used and that it was an endearment which held no significance.

Although her sleep was short and restless, Sarah awoke the next morning at her usual time and joined her aunt for breakfast. After apologizing again for her previous night's behavior, she told Mrs. Mashburne the details of her conversation with Lady Waxton. "I suppose it was the hurt and anger over Judith's daring to set someone to spy upon me which caused me to so forget the proprieties as to accept a third waltz with Ravenwilde. That, I mean, on top of..." She hesitated and then stopped. She could not admit her love for Ravenwilde to Aunt Silvia, for she could not bear the pity she knew would result from disclosing her feelings. "How could she possibly do such a thing?" she continued. "I know her to be insensitive, but I never dreamed she would stoop to *spying,* and to engage the assistance of one such as Lady Waxton is the outside of enough. She has gone too far this time, Aunt Silvia, and so I shall tell her when next we meet."

"I agree, my love," her aunt answered, "but our immediate concern is to minimize the consequences of your actions. I have given the matter some thought and I think our best course of action is to simply go on as we have as if nothing had happened. I can think of nothing else to do at the moment." She did not see fit to disclose to Sarah her fears that they would be given the cut direct from many members of the ton.

"No, nor can I," Sarah admitted. "I am truly sorry, dear Aunt, to have embroiled you in this unpleasant affair. You were not to blame, but there are those who will say you were, since you are my companion."

"And they will be right," Mrs. Mashburne replied. "I should have stayed close enough to you to prevent such a thing. Instead, I was enjoying myself with Mr. Brooks."

"Please do not blame yourself," Sarah pleaded with tears in her eyes. "I simply cannot bear to see you hurt over something I have done."

"Never mind, love," Mrs. Mashburne answered, leading Sarah from the table into the Morning Saloon. "We shall come about, see if we don't."

They were no sooner settled than Stevens announced the dowager Duchess of Bloomington. Sarah and Mrs. Mashburne looked at each other in astonishment. It was a well-known fact that the duchess rarely left her home, and never left her bedchamber before noon.

Forgetting her own problems, Sarah rose and hurried across the room to greet the old lady. Holding out both hands, she said, "My dear ma'am, how good to see you," and studying the old lady's face she continued, "I do hope nothing is amiss?"

Allowing Sarah to kiss her on the cheek, the duchess said, "Nothing with *me,* my dear, but I fear it is far otherwise with *you.* You must know that the Waxton woman's tongue has been busy. I have just this past hour been informed of last night's misadventure and would have summoned my scapegrace of a grandson at once, but was handed a letter from him with my morning chocolate advising me that he would be out of town for a few days."

A pain, almost physical, jolted Sarah in the region of her heart. So the duke had abandoned her to face the gossips alone.

Reaching into her reticule, the duchess handed Sarah a letter. "Here, child, this is for you. Harry asked that I deliver it. Go on, read it."

"Thank you, ma'am," Sarah said, and begging the pardon of both her aunt and the duchess, she walked over to the window to read her message in private. "Dearest Sarah," she read, "I have asked my grandmother to deliver this to you since I found it necessary to leave very early this morning. Since I cannot be with you for the next few days, I have asked her to stand with you against the storm my rash and unforgivable action last night is certain to bring. She will know better than I what to do to smooth things over, and when I return, I hope to bring with me tidings which will make everything all right again. Until then, I am your faithful servant in all things. R."

Whatever could he mean, and where had he gone? "Did Ravenwilde tell you where he was going, ma'am?" Sarah asked the duchess.

"No," she replied, "only that he would be away for a few days and that, in his absence, I was to do what I could to help you through the muddle he has caused. Not that he had to ask me to do it, for you must know, my little friend, that I would have come to you immediately I heard that you needed me."

Tears welled up in Sarah's eyes again as she clasped the old lady's hand. "Oh, dear ma'am, I do not deserve such a friend as you."

"Perhaps not," the old lady replied with a twinkle in her sharp blue eyes, "but then if we all got what we deserve, most of us would be in hell with our backs broken."

In spite of her problems, an involuntary gurgle of laughter escaped Sarah's throat. "Oh, ma'am, if I may say so without seeming impertinent, you are the most complete hand."

"Saucy puss," the duchess replied affectionately.

At that moment, Stevens announced Lady Ainsberry, who, after properly greeting the duchess and Mrs. Mashburne, took both Sarah's hands in her own and said, "My dearest friend, tell me what I may do to help. I have just this hour heard, and I felt I must come to you at once." Turning to the duchess, she said, "Your grace, I am so pleased to find you here. I was going to make so bold as to call upon you when I left Sarah this morning," adding with a sweet smile, "and that was brave of me, indeed, knowing as all the ton does that you are loath to be disturbed so early in the morning."

"I am surrounded by sassy misses," the duchess retorted, "but I need not scruple to tell you, Margaret, that I am glad you are here. I think that if the two of *us* are seen to be on friendly terms with Sarah, no one else will dare cut her. *Our* credit can stand much more than this little tempest in a teacup," she finished grandly.

"Indeed, yes," Lady Ainsberry agreed.

"Now," the duchess said, "what I propose is that the three of us ride together in the park in *my* carriage this afternoon. You will not mind being left out, will you, Silvia? For this first outing, I think it better that you stay out of sight. We in this room know it to be untrue, but there are those who will lay some blame on your shoulders for last night's breach of the proprieties, since you are in some way Sarah's chaperon."

"Of course not, ma'am. I am happy to do your bidding in all things."

"And you, miss," the duchess said, pinning Sarah with her piercing eyes, "will be seen wearing your most dashing outfit. You will not apologize, either by word or bearing, for what has occurred. You will comport yourself in your usual manner, neither groveling nor defiant. Tomorrow morning you will ride horseback accompanied by Margaret. I am too old for horseback riding, but I will be in the park in my carriage and make a point of speaking to you. You will also further indulge an old lady by wearing that dashing red velvet habit I saw you in a few weeks back; the one with the matching hat with white ostrich feathers. On Tuesday night we shall all attend the masquerade at Vauxhall Gardens. In the normal way of things, I do not approve of such affairs, but this, you will admit, is not a normal circumstance. I shall be thinking on other things to do which will scotch this gossip before it goes too far. Already I have sent out invitations to a few key leaders of the ton to partake of tea and biscuits with me late this afternoon after our ride. Short notice, I know, but I have no doubt they will *all* attend. That will give me an excellent opportunity to line up the big guns on our side. Now I must take my leave of you ladies. I have things to do."

Thus saying, the old lady stood up and marched majestically toward the door, saying as she pulled on her gloves, "Ravenwilde should be back by Wednesday, so you may expect an offer of marriage on that date."

"Indeed I will not! Sarah responded sharply.

Laughing softly, the old lady said, "That's the ticket, my dear. Spirit. Spirit is what it will take to see us through this thing. Until this afternoon, ladies," and with that she marched grandly through the door which Mrs. Mashburne had opened for her.

"Well," Sarah sighed, "I am excessively glad she is a *friend* of mine. I should hate to have her for an *enemy.*"

"Indeed yes," Lady Ainsberry agreed laughingly. "I will now take my leave of you also, dear Sarah. Should you find you need me before we meet this afternoon, please send for me."

"Thank you, Margaret. You are much too good to me," Sarah replied tearfully. "I do not know what has come over me. I was never used to be a watering pot, but just lately I find myself tearing up for no apparent reason at all. I, who hate a weeping woman above all things, am in grave danger of becoming one myself."

"I do not think it, my dear," Lady Ainsberry replied gently. "It is only that you have been under a great deal of strain lately. Everything will turn out all right; wait and see."

And everything did go smoothly until the third day, when Sarah returned from riding with Lady Ainsberry to find Judith and the despised pug established in her drawing room with a red-eyed Mrs. Mashburne.

"Judith," she exclaimed, "whatever brings you to London?"

"Well you might ask," Judith replied angrily. "News of your disgraceful behavior has reached all the way to the country. I could scarcely believe my ears, and when dear Randolph and I discussed the matter, we concluded that there was nothing for me to do but tear myself away from my home and dear husband and journey to London to see what could be done. I did warn you, you know, what would happen if you persisted in your ill-advised scheme to set up your own place, and now that you have made a cake of yourself and seriously damaged your reputation, I had to come to you, causing myself and my household a great deal of inconvenience."

Sarah felt her anger rising by the minute, but managed to say calmly, "You have wasted your time, Judith. I have no need of you. You can do yourself as well as me a favor by posting back home with all possible speed."

Much astonished, Judith said, "What? How can you say you have no need of me? You certainly must have *someone* to lend you countenance at this time."

"I have someone," Sarah replied. "Aunt Silvia is still with me, you know."

"Silvia!" Judith spat out the name as she would a foul-tasting potent. "Far from lending you countenance, her behavior is almost as bad as yours. Do not think it has not reached my notice that she is gallivanting all over town in the company of Mr. Brooks. While posing as your companion and chaperon, she has had the nerve to steal your suitor from beneath your very nose. She is a brass-faced hussy, and I have already told her so."

"Indeed!" Sarah ejaculated. "And what, pray tell, gives you the right to come into *my* home and insult *my* guest? I demand that you apologize to her at once."

"No, please, Sarah," Mrs. Mashburne cried. "Please do not fight over me."

"I shall indeed fight over you, Aunt Silvia," Sarah said, and turning to Judith she said, "I am waiting for your apology, Judith."

"I will not," Judith answered.

"Then you will be so kind as to leave my house at once," Sarah answered, ringing for Stevens. When he appeared she said, "My sister is leaving, Steven. Please see her to her carriage."

"You cannot do this thing, Sarah," Judith cried, dropping the pug to the floor, where Casper took immediate exception to his presence and began to growl threateningly. The pug showed better sense than his mistress and retreated behind the sofa. "I have already had my baggage installed in the rose bedroom, and little Charles has been put to bed to rest after the journey. Poor darling, he was so tired."

"Your baggage as well as Charles's comfort are matters of supreme indifference to me, Judith, but Aunt Silvia's feelings are of paramount importance. You will apologize to her immediately or leave my home."

Becoming braver after having routed the pug so easily, Casper decided to seek him out in his hiding place. A series of growls and yaps and barks was heard from behind the couch, and with a shriek, Judith began moving the couch in order to get to her pug.

"And you will be so kind as to restrain that odious dog of yours," Sarah continued, blithely ignoring the fact that Casper was the aggressor. "He is almost as bad-mannered as he is ugly."

"How dare you!" Judith cried.

"I shall dare anything I like in my own home," Sarah retorted, "and I am still waiting for you to apologize to Aunt Silvia, but I warn you, I do not intend to wait much longer. Now, Judith!"

"Very well, Silvia, I am sorry if I offended you. Perhaps the intelligence I received was in error."

"No," Sarah replied, "it was not in error. Aunt Silvia and Mr. Brooks are to be married, with my full approval and blessings. They will make a wonderful couple and I am very happy for her."

"Well, really, Sarah, what strange behavior, to be sure."

"Not strange at all, Judith. They are two lovely people who met and fell in love. Nothing could be more unexceptionable. The behavior I find strange and cannot forgive is your own, sister. How dare you set Lady Waxton to spy upon me! You went much too far, Judith, and I warn you I shall never forgive you. That was contemptible—nay, that was beneath contempt."

"Your very own actions proved it was necessary, Sarah. You cannot deny that you placed yourself beyond the pale."

"Perhaps I acted with less discretion than I should have, Judith, but I was so angry when Lady Waxton told me you had engaged her to keep an eye on me that I was not responsible for my actions. That coupled with another matter I had on my mind at the time was the outside of enough. I was blinded by anger and hurt. To think that my own sister would do such a thing to me left me no power to act rationally. I lay the whole thing at your door, and you can be thankful that I could not get my hands on you that night."

"Are you threatening me, Sarah?" Judith asked, aghast.

"No, merely advising you to stay out of my affairs. I neither want nor need your interference. I am tired now. I am going to lie down for a while." After opening the door she turned and said, "And please make a point of keeping your dog and your son away from me. Just now I do not think I can be responsible if either of them gets in my way."

"Oh, that reminds me, Sarah. Your footman was positively rude to little Charles. You really must speak to him."

"I shall do no such thing," Sarah retorted, unaware that Stevens and several other servants were standing in the hall awaiting her instructions concerning the guests. "And I will take this opportunity to remind you that the servants in this house are not only *my* servants, but they are old and valued friends as well and are to be treated as such by you and Charles. Papa saw to it before he died that all those servants who had befriended me when I was a child were transferred to this house and to Foxborough. I am sure he knew I would have need of their support and friendship, for I cannot depend upon my sister. Keep that in mind, Judith, for if I must make a choice, that choice will be ridiculously easy. You will *not* treat my servants as you treat your own. They are to be treated with kindness and consideration. Do I make myself clear?"

So saying, she left the room followed by the victorious Casper, leaving behind several happy servants who wasted no time in relating to the other members of the household the words of their beloved mistress.

Oblivious to the fact that the servants had heard her words to Judith, Sarah made her way to her own bedchamber, and after removing her gown, she drew the curtains and lay down, hoping an hour's rest would relieve the stress and tension Judith's arrival had caused to build within her.

Until her sister's arrival, everything had gone according to the duchess's plans. When it was seen by the ton that the duchess and Lady Ainsberry, as well as other leaders of the ton (influenced by the duchess), were not cutting her, the lesser members, with a few exceptions whom the duchess airly dismissed as of no importance, fell into line. Although Sarah had determined that she would not spend another whole season in London, she knew it would be unbearable to be shunned by the ton. She might make light of some of the rules and privately chafe against some restrictions placed upon her, but in her heart she knew those things were important to a lady of quality. She was born into a certain way of life and had no desire to be forced to live on the fringes of the society which she had always taken for granted. She felt an enormous gratitude toward the duchess and Lady Ainsberry, for she knew that without their help, she and her aunt would never have been able to see the thing through with any appreciable success.

But where was Ravenwilde, and what did he mean when he wrote that he would return with tidings that would make everything all right? What tidings? Neither she nor the duchess had heard anything from him since the day he left, and Sarah was beginning to feel a little uneasy. He had left so abruptly that no one, and surely that included his enemy, could know where he was. The duchess had made inquiries at his home and been told that he had not left with any of the servants any intelligence as to his destination. He had left a note for his butler instructing him to deliver certain letters to the duchess, but beyond that, no one in his household knew any more than did Sarah and the duchess.

Sarah was very much relieved when the duchess did not approach the subject of Ravenwilde's making her an offer again, and soon was convinced that she had merely mentioned it that once in order to raise Sarah's spirits. Sarah was sure the duchess knew her well enough to know she would never, under any circumstances, accept an offer made under such conditions. She had made it quite clear to the duchess and everyone else that Ravenwilde was not responsible for her present predicament. "For you must know, ma'am," Sarah had said to the duchess, "that I am no schoolroom miss to be led astray. I am fully aware of the rules of society, probably more so than Ravenwilde, and should have been more on my guard. Indeed, obeying the rules should be so much a part of me by now, for I am all of seven and twenty, that I should be able to carry on without even thinking about them. I cannot imagine how I came to be so lax as to forget, even for one moment."

The duchess did not answer, but exchanged a shrewd look with Lady Ainsberry. Neither lady had voiced her opinions as to the state of Sarah's emotions, but both had their suspicions that Sarah was in love with Ravenwilde and both wondered when Sarah herself would realize that fact. They had no way of knowing that she had already admitted as much, for she was keeping her private feelings very much to herself.

Finally she was able to fall into an easy sleep, and she awoke very much refreshed. While dressing for dinner, she promised herself that she would not come to cuffs with Judith again but would bear her presence with equanimity until Judith saw she was neither needed nor wanted and returned to her own home. If she was determined to stay in London for any length of time, Sarah would suggest that she open her own house and remove herself, her dog, her child, and her servants to it. As much as she was loath to fight with Judith, she had no intention of putting up with her for the rest of the season.

Thus fortified with good intentions and firm resolve, she left her room and descended the stairs to endure what she hoped would be a short evening with her sister.

The night of the masquerade ball at Vauxhall

Gardens was marked by a full moon and crisp, cool air. Sarah, accompanied by her aunt and Mr. Brooks, met the duchess and Lord and Lady Ainsberry at a prearranged spot and proceeded on to the box Lord Ainsberry had previously bespoken. The ladies, with the exception of the duchess, who adamantly refused to wear any sort of disguise, were dressed in dominos and masks. Sarah's domino was bright green and her black mask was encrusted with sparkling rhinestones. Lady Ainsberry wore red and Mrs. Mashburne was in black. Both men wore black-and-white checked dominos and black masks.

Since the duchess was not in costume, everyone present was able to recognize her companions immediately, and soon their box was crowded with people who did not want to waste an opportunity to be seen in such august company. Sarah smiled behind her fan, reflecting once again that rank and wealth certainly carried a great deal of weight in their society, but this time she was grateful that those who possessed the rank and wealth were on her side. It was true that she had been born into an old and respected family and that her own consequences were great, but it was also true that while her own background was more than respectable, it could not match that of the duchess and Lady Ainsberry, and while the storm over her behavior a week or so past had begun to wane, she knew she was still very much in need of the protection the friendship of those two ladies afforded.

The duchess had instructed Sarah to act naturally, to talk and dance and visit with friends and acquaintances as if nothing had happened, so it was with a great deal of pleasure that she accepted the invitations to dance from several of the young men who approached her. However, she was very much surprised and a little vexed when an unfamiliar gentleman wearing a black domino and black mask cut in on the young man who had led her onto the dance floor. Such things were common at masquerade balls, but it had never happened to Sarah, and she was not pleased to find herself dancing with someone who had not first been approved by the duchess, especially at this particular time.

Before Sarah could protest, the gentleman said, "It is I, Donnelly, Miss Windemere, and I have a message from Ravenwilde for you."

"Ravenwilde?" Sarah asked in some alarm. "Where is he? Is he all right?"

Smoothly Donnelly answered, "Well, that is a matter of opinion. He asked me to tell you that he needs you and that if you consent to come to him, he also charged that I should see that you arrive safely."

"I thank you for bringing me his message, sir, but it will not be necessary to put you to the trouble of accompanying me. If you will but give me his direction, I shall seek out Lord Ainsberry and ask that he accompany me. You must know that they are the best of friends, and if Ravenwilde is in some sort of trouble, I feel sure he will be glad of Lord Ainsberry's assistance."

"In the normal way of things, I am sure you are right, Miss Windemere, but I must tell you that this is not an *ordinary* circumstance. Ravenwilde specifically asked that I tell no one except you and that I beg you to come to him alone. He instructed me that on no account should *anyone* else be brought into the matter and that if you decline his request, I am to return alone."

Although Sarah was bewildered by such a request, she knew that Ravenwilde would never ask her to do such an unconventional thing if it were not very important to him. Still she hesitated. "I shall have to tell the duchess that I am leaving."

"No!" Donnelly answered sharply. "If you go, you must go at once. I cannot leave him alone much longer. Our little journey will not take long, and I shall have you back before the duchess misses you. He specifically mentioned that he did not want his grandmother to worry. Come, you must make up your mind; he cannot wait much longer."

Knowing well Ravenwilde's concern for his grandmother, Sarah felt that Donnelly's words held a ring of truth and answered, "Very well, but let us make haste. I cannot be away long."

She allowed herself to be helped into what was obviously a hired carriage. The brief glimpse she got of the rough man driving the mismatched team of horses was vaguely familiar, but so great was her concern for Ravenwilde that she lost little time trying to remember where she had seen him.

"Where is Ravenwilde," she asked when they were on their way, "and what kind of trouble is he in?"

"You will see soon enough," Donnelly answered, rather smugly Sarah thought.

After some thirty minutes, the coach pulled up at a rather shabby cottage on the outskirts of London, and Donnelly, after instructing his driver to keep a close watch, led Sarah into an equally shabby and poorly lighted room. Straining to see into the shadows of the room, she called, "Ravenwilde, where are you?"

"He will be here soon, my dear," Donnelly said. "Just make yourself comfortable."

A twinge of fear was beginning to be felt by Sarah, but her voice was steady as she turned on Donnelly to say, "You told me he would be here. Where is he? Why have you lied to me?"

"Do not despair, he will be here. You see, I left a note at his home telling him where you would be. He will waste no time in coming to you."

"You must be mad!" Sarah stormed. "Ravenwilde is out of town and no one knows when he will return. You have wasted your time, sir, and put me in a most awkward position, all for naught. I have no intention of staying here another minute. I am returning to the ball at once. Perhaps my absence has not been noted."

Thus saying, she opened the door through which they had entered only to find the man who had driven the coach blocking her path. Looking into his menacing face, she felt a fear and horror such as she had never before felt. Her legs felt weak, and one hand fluttered ineffectually in the region of her fast-beating heart. The man she now recognized was one of those who had attacked Ravenwilde in the gardens. Turning to face Donnelly, she whispered hoarsely, "You! It was you who tried to have Ravenwilde killed!"

Chapter 10

"Ah, yes," Donnelly answered calmly. "A most unfortunate necessity, I assure you. I never *wanted* to harm him, but he *would* come home, and at a most inconvenient time for me."

"I do not understand," Sarah said, sinking onto a nearby chair. She felt as if her legs would no longer support her.

"It is really quite simple, my dear," Donnelly explained. "As Ravenwilde's heir, I was able to live quite handsomely on my expectations. However, when he came home, obviously in excellent health and looking very much like a man who planned to marry and set up his nursery, my creditors got worried and began to dun me. I appealed to Ravenwilde for assistance, and must admit that he did advance me rather a large sum of money, but not nearly enough. Can you imagine how much of the ready it takes for a man to live these days?" Thus saying, he laughed harshly, causing a sinking feeling in the pit of Sarah's stomach. The man was mad; there was no other explanation for his actions.

"I am sure Ravenwilde would help you if you but explained the whole to him," Sarah said in an effort to placate him.

Turning on her angrily, Donnelly said, "Do not be too sure, Miss Windemere. I did explain the whole to him and he told me he would not give me another groat so long as I stayed in England. He said he had no intention of seeing me waste away the whole of his inheritance; that he had every intention of having children of his own and that he had an obligation to his future heirs. Oh, he did offer to pay my passage to America and advance me enough money to get a start there, but I have no desire to leave England. I shall have what I need right here."

"But how?" Sarah asked. "If Ravenwilde has refused you once, he surely will refuse you again."

"Yes," Donnelly answered with a wicked smile. "I fully realize that. That is why I decided that I had to kill him. The stupid idiots I hired to do the job for me failed miserably. Now I have decided to do the thing myself."

"But I told you Ravenwilde is out of town." Sarah cried.

"No, my dear, he is back. I have had his house watched, and early this very evening I was informed that he had returned. I then sent a message around to his house to inform him that I had *you* and that if he wanted to see you again alive and, uh, unharmed, he would, without delay, present himself here, alone."

"What do you plan to do with us?" Sarah asked, knowing what the ultimate answer would be but morbidly curious as to how he planned to kill them. "You cannot possibly hope to get away with killing us both."

At that he laughed and said, "Of course I hope to get away with it. I have given the matter a great deal of thought. You would be surprised how cunning a man faced with imprisonment for failing to pay his debts can be. Of course, you and Ravenwilde aided me immediately. It is obvious to all of London that he is in love with you. Your own feelings are a little harder to divine, but after the little scandal you recently created, what would be more natural than for him to make you an offer and for you to accept? Naturally, neither of you would want a fuss made over your marriage, so you decided to elope to Gretna Green. I shall put you on the road to the border in a hired coach, shoot you both, and relieve you of your jewelry and Ravenwilde of his purse, and when you are found, it will look to all the world as though you were robbed and killed while trying to elope to the border."

Sarah sat in stunned silence as she absorbed what Donnelly was saying. He was right. It would work. With mounting horror, she realized that after her recent scandalous behavior and Ravenwilde's past reputation (however undeserved, and anyway, few *knew* that it was undeserved), most people would believe that they had eloped and many would say that their fate was appropriate.

"Oh, God," she prayed silently, "please do not let him come."

"It is too bad you had to be involved in this, Miss Windemere. I have no quarrel with you, but when my first two attempts failed, I knew I had to devise a foolproof plan, and that is where you came in."

"He will not come," Sarah said. "You are quite mistaken about his feelings for me. Ravenwilde cares naught for me."

Even as she spoke the words, and believed them, she had a sinking feeling in the region of her heart. As much as she had wanted him to love her before, she now hoped with all her heart and soul that he would callously turn aside from Donnelly's note and tell himself that what happened to her was no concern of his. It would make no difference to her, for she knew that whatever Ravenwilde did now, Donnelly had to kill her. She knew too much. "Do not let him come," she prayed again, but even as she whispered the words, she heard a carriage enter the deserted street and saw a look of smug satisfaction on Donnelly's face.

"Ah," he breathed, "here he is now, and how fortunate that he brought a carriage. Now I can send you on your final journey in Ravenwilde's own carriage. The hired carriage being traced to me was the only worry I had, and Ravenwilde has been so obliging as to remove that concern from my mind." Thus saying, he picked up a pistol which was lying on a nearby table and pointed it at the door.

No sooner did Ravenwilde's large shoulders fill the doorway than Sarah cried, "Oh, Ravenwilde, why did you come? Could you not guess it was a trap?"

Sarah had never seen him look so grim. No longer was there laughter in his brown eyes. Now they held a look of cold steel. There was a white circle around his sensuous mouth and a firm set to his strong jaw. His eyes pierced her face as he asked grimly, "Are you all right, Sarah?"

"Yes," she whispered. She had been right; he cared

naught for her. There was not the slightest softening of his features or his voice when he looked at and spoke to her. If only she had not been so stupid as to accompany Donnelly, none of this would have happened.

"Well, Donnelly," Ravenwilde was saying, "and what are your plans now? Will you kill us here or take us someplace else?"

"One of the things I most admire about you, cousin, is your quick assessment of any situation," Donnelly answered dryly. "I shall, of course, take you someplace else. I was just explaining to Miss Windemere that I shall set you on the road to the border, kill you, and make it look as if you were robbed and murdered while eloping."

"Allow me to congratulate you," Ravenwilde said calmly. "That is a remarkably well thought-out plan—unlike the first two."

"Yes, it is, isn't it?" Donnelly replied with satisfaction. "I made the mistake of relying on someone else the first two times. It is sad but true if one wants a thing done well, he must undertake to do it himself."

"Then you intend to accompany us on our little journey alone?"

Donnelly smiled a smile that chilled Sarah's heart before he answered. "Yes, but do not think to overpower me, Ravenwilde. *You* shall drive and I will keep the charming Miss Windemere company inside the coach. My pistol will be pointed at her lovely head at all times, and, as you already know, I will have nothing to lose by pulling the trigger. And make no mistake, I shall not hesitate to do so if you should try anything foolish."

"I do not doubt it for a moment," Ravenwilde replied.

"Then shall we go? The night is already far advanced, and I hope to be back in my own bed before dawn."

"Oh, that reminds me," Ravenwilde said, "how do you suppose to get home afterward? Surely you do not mean to walk."

Donnelly laughed with real amusement. "Walk? Me? Of course not! I have already tied a horse in a thicket beside the road we shall travel. I shan't take you far beyond where he is tied."

"It seems you have thought of everything," Ravenwilde said.

"Of course, dear cousin, even as to how I intend to spend a great deal of your money. Now, shall we go? You first, Ravenwilde, and remember that my pistol is pointed at your dear Sarah's back."

As they began to walk slowly toward the door, Sarah suddenly realized what she must do. Donnelly had only one shot in the pistol he was holding, and there were two of them. If she could force him to discharge the pistol, he would be defenseless, and she knew he would be no match for Ravenwilde in a fistfight. Of course there was a danger, but the most danger was to herself, and if she had not been so stupid as to accompany Donnelly, Ravenwilde would not now be in danger. They were to die anyway, and in her present state of mind, she decided that one place was as good as another to die. Turning quickly to face Donnelly, she cried, "No, you shall not do this to him," as she grabbed for the hand which held the gun. They struggled for a moment before Sarah heard a loud blast and felt a searing, burning pain in the region of her shoulder and saw Ravenwilde lunge for Donnelly and swing a powerful fist toward his face.

She sank very slowly to the floor, conscious only

of the burning pain in her shoulder until Ravenwilde knelt beside her and cradled her gently in his arms. "Oh, Sarah, why did you do it? Did you not know I would not have come without making arrangements for your rescue?"

Although her mind was numbed by pain, she was conscious of a movement behind Ravenwilde and saw through pain-filled eyes Donnelly approaching with a knife in his upraised hand. She tried to warn Ravenwilde, but only gurgling sounds escaped her throat. The knife was descending toward Ravenwilde's back when she became aware of the door bursting open and again heard the loud report of a pistol. She saw through glazed eyes Lord Ainsberry standing in the door holding a smoking pistol, and managed a weak smile at Ravenwilde before merciful blackness blocked out the pain.

Some time later she was again aware of the excruciating pain in her shoulder. She did not know the doctor was probing for the embedded pistol ball, or that Ravenwilde and Lord Ainsberry, along with Mrs. Mashburne, were assisting him. Nor could she know that the pain Ravenwilde was feeling as he held her on the bed was almost as great as her own. All she knew was that all the fires of hell were burning in her shoulder, and she wondered briefly, before blackness engulfed her again, if she had indeed died and gone to hell.

It was two days before she regained consciousness to see Mrs. Mashburne hovering over her bed. She tried to speak, but her mouth and lips were too parched to allow coherent words. Cooing softly, Mrs. Mashburne wet her dry lips with a cloth and squeezed a few drops of water into her mouth. When she was able, Sarah whispered, "Ravenwilde?" And when her aunt assured her that he was well, she slipped back into darkness, but her aunt was pleased and relieved to note that this time, it was sleep and not unconsciousness.

Leaving Sarah with her maid, Mrs. Mashburne slipped down to the Morning Saloon to report to the duchess, Lady Ainsberry, and Ravenwilde that Sarah was better. The four of them had kept a constant vigil, each lost in his own feelings of horror, grief, and guilt. Each of the ladies blamed herself for not keeping a closer watch over her, and Ravenwilde blamed himself for being the cause of her being in such a dangerous situation. Judith wandered in from time to time to complain bitterly about a sister who was so lost to the proprieties as to allow herself to become embroiled in such a situation. She chose the time when Mrs. Mashburne was relating Sarah's improvement to make one of her infrequent appearances and was unwise enough to say, "Well, I must say it is more than she deserves. A more willful girl I have never seen. If she had but listened to older and wiser heads, none of this would have happened."

"You're a dammed fool, Judith!" the duchess said scathingly. "You always were."

"Really, ma'am," Judith protested, "she *is* my sister, and I think I know her better than anyone else."

"You don't know anything," the duchess said. "You never did. We are all of us aware that Sarah is your sister, and each of us marvels at it."

"I'll say no more, ma'am," Judith said primly, "only to add that as soon as she is able, I shall remove her to the country. There she will remain until she is safely married. Not that I expect her to make much of a match *now*, but she is, after all, the possessor of a handsome fortune, and a *respectable* match shouldn't be to difficult to arrange. Of course, she has flittered away any chance she might have had for a really good match and now must be content to take what she can get."

Speaking up, Mrs. Mashburne retorted, "I think what Sarah decides to do when she is well is a thing we should leave until she *is* well. I am sure she will have some ideas on that subject herself. I know she was planning to go to Foxborough at the end of the season, and I strongly think she will want to go there when she is well enough to travel." '

"Well, we'll see about that," Judith answered smugly. "Surely this latest escapade of hers has drummed some sense into her. Randolph and I consider it our Christian as well as familial duty to take her in, regardless of the scandal she has created."

"Pish posh," the duchess spat, thus effectively ending the conversation.

Sarah suffered several more days of pain and fever before she began to heal. When she began to feel well enough, Mrs. Mashburne allowed a few select friends to make short visits to the sickroom. Of course, the duchess and Lady Ainsberry visited as often as they wanted, and they took turns sitting with her while Silvia took brief walks in the fresh air or rested for an hour or so in her room. Sarah soon noticed that her aunt was looking tired and insisted that she spend less time with her and more time resting or riding in the park with Mr. Brooks. "For you must know, dear Aunt, that I am well on the road to recovery now and have no need to be watched over constantly. Besides, I hate to have a fuss made over me, as you are well aware. Now, love, do me a favor and go lie down for a while. I promise you that if I have need of you, I will ring at once."

The season came to an end, and almost everyone left London. Sarah was still not strong enough to travel; in point of fact, she had not yet left her room.

The doctor reluctantly allowed her to sit up on a couch in her sitting room, but still had not allowed her to venture downstairs. Actually she had had no desire to go down. Mrs. Mashburne had told her that Ravenwilde called every day to inquire about her health, and she had no desire to meet him just yet. She knew that a meeting between the two of them was inevitable, but she wanted to postpone that time for as long as possible. She still felt a complete idiot for having fallen into such a trap as Donnelly had set for them, and was bothered by feelings of guilt for having put Ravenwilde's life in danger.

However, when the duchess visited her on a dreary early December day and informed her that she was leaving for her country estate the next day and that Ravenwilde would accompany her, Sarah decided it was safe to venture downstairs. The duchess had told her, "I have persuaded Harry to stay with me until after Christmas. He was reluctant to leave town while you are still abed, but I persuaded him that it would be much better for him to be away from London until such time as you are well enough to venture out again. He has wanted very much to see you, you know, but is being guided by your aunt's opinion that it would be better to wait until you are downstairs again."

Sarah felt a slight flush creeping into her face and turned away in an effort to hide her expression from the duchess. "Really, ma'am, there is no need for Ravenwilde to see me. He has been all that is kind, and I do appreciate it, but I am sure he has far better things to do than to cool his heels waiting for me to get well. He needs to get on with his own plans and forget about my accident. It was entirely my own fault; no blame can possibly be placed on his shoulders, and I would feel much better if I knew he had put the whole thing out of his mind. Please inform him of my wishes, will you, ma'am?"

"Of course, dear child," the duchess answered gently. "I wish I could persuade you to come to me for a period of recuperation. I would make you very welcome and comfortable, you know."

"Oh, yes, I do know, and am more grateful than you can possibly know. However, when I am able to travel, I shall return to Foxborough. Be assured that I shall write to you and we will no doubt meet again next season."

"That is too far ahead for an old woman like me to plan, my dear, but we shall see."

It was not many days before Lady Ainsberry also informed Sarah that she was leaving London to prepare for Christmas at their family seat. "I do hate leaving you alone, dear Sarah, but I must plan Christmas for the children and Oliver. You do understand, don't you?"

"Of course I understand, Margaret. I can never repay you for your kindness to me, but please know that I am grateful. I shan't be alone, you know. Aunt Silvia is staying with me until I am well enough to travel to Foxborough. I feel such a wretch tying her down this way, but I cannot and will not stay with Judith. Besides, she is returning to the country in a few days to spend Christmas there. Frankly, I shall be glad to have her out of the house. She is a great trial to me and Aunt Silvia."

"You know you can always come to me," Lady Ainsberry said. "I should be glad to welcome you at any time, and be assured that Oliver feels the same."

"I know, dear friend, and I appreciate it. I shall keep in touch and let you know my plans."

It had been a week since the duchess and Ravenwilde had departed London, and Sarah, though dispirited, felt physically well enough to join Mrs. Mashburne and Judith in the dining room for dinner. It was to be Judith's last night in London, as she too planned to depart for the country to prepare for Christmas with her family. "I shall return immediately after Boxing Day to escort you to the country if the weather permits," Judith had informed Sarah imperiously, and for the first time in her life, Sarah found herself wishing for a snowstorm which would render the roads impassable. She had told Judith that her plans were to remove to Foxborough as soon as she was strong enough to travel, but as usual, Judith had ignored any plans which did not suit her own and Sarah did not feel well enough either physically or emotionally to enter into an argument over the matter. Consequently, Judith felt she had won a victory, and Mrs. Mashburne marveled once again at her older niece's stupidity. She knew well that long before Judith returned to London, Sarah would have departed for Foxborough and was secretly amused when she considered Judith's rage when she again set down in Brook Street only to find the knocker removed from the door.

After dinner, when the ladies were sitting in front of a roaring fire drinking tea, Judith asked, "And where is your Mr. Brooks, Silvia? I haven't seen him around here lately. Has he abandoned you already?"

In spite of Judith's nasty remark, Mrs. Mashburne answered sweetly, "He, too, has departed for his family seat to spend Christmas with his family. We agreed, he and I, that I should stay with Sarah until such time as she is able to travel and that he should take this opportunity to make known to his son our wedding plans. We shall be married from his home in the spring, quietly, with only family and very close friends in attendance."

"Well," Judith replied nastily, "I'm sure I wish you happy. However, how you can be satisfied with a man who dangled after Sarah for an age and only chose *you* when it became apparent that she would not have him is more than I can tell."

"That's enough, Judith," Sarah said sharply. "We all of us know that Mr. Brooks was never seriously interested in me. He only called upon me out of lonliness, and I was the only eligible lady near. But here in London it was quite another thing, and out of all the ladies dangling after him, he chose Aunt Silvia. It was obvious even to the meanest intelligence that he loved her almost from the beginning. They are perfectly suited and I am very happy for them."

Only a little chastised, Judith replied, "Well, and what about you, miss? Dangling after Ravenwilde like a moonstruck schoolroom miss! I never have been so embarrassed in all my life. To think that a sister of mine would be so lost to the proprieties as to involve herself with a man of his reputation."

So heated was the discussion that none of the ladies heard the door to the saloon open softly, nor were they aware of the tall figure leaning negligently against the door he had made sure to close as softly as he had opened it.

When Ravenwilde had presented himself to Stevens, he had assured that loyal servant that there was no need for him to announce him. Stevens, as he related to the rest of the household later, knew a man in love when he saw one, and he, for one, thought the Duke of Ravenwilde a very fine gentleman and *just* the man to bring his beloved mistress out of her glooms, and that was why he had allowed the duke his way. And besides, what could he, an old man, do against Ravenwilde's strength? And seeing the determination in the gentleman's eyes, he knew it was useless to cross him, even if he had been so inclined, which he wasn't. So there! This tangled speech was delivered rather belligerently below-stairs while quite another drama was being enacted above.

"Stop it, Judith," Sarah replied angrily. "I will not have you disparage Ravenwilde. Nothing that has happened is any fault of his. He has always comported himself as he ought. The blame is mine."

Taken aback by her sister's vehement defense of Ravenwilde, Judith said, "I do believe you are in love with the man."

"Yes," Sarah answered dreamily, "I am."

"What?" Judith cried, surprised even though she had suspected the truth. "And what will you do now?"

"Do? Now? Why nothing," Sarah replied calmly. "That is, I shall do nothing out of the ordinary. I shall simply return to Foxborough and begin learning how to manage a country estate."

"But what of marriage?" Judith asked.

"You must know that marriage is out of the question for me, Judith. Indeed, I think it always was. I was no doubt born to be a spinster," Sarah answered softly.

"Oh, my dear," Mrs. Mashburne cried, "I am so very sorry."

"Shush now, Aunt Silvia. You must promise not to worry about me, nor are you to feel sorry for me. I have known such moments of pure delight as I doubt many married ladies have ever experienced. All my memories are sweet, and I do assure you that I would rather live with those memories of Raven-wilde than to live the rest of my life with another man."

"You're a fool, Sarah," Judith said scathingly, "and you can't say I didn't warn you. That very first day I warned you about him."

"It was already too late, Judith," Sarah answered with a sweet smile. "I think I loved him from the moment he stepped into my life and I looked into his laughing brown eyes. No, perhaps it was when he threw back his head and laughed that I fell in love with him. Ah, I really do not know the exact moment, but I do know it was during that first encounter. So you see, Judith, your warning came much too late and it would not have mattered anyway. The only thing that matters is that I *do* love him and shall do so for the rest of my life. I am not a child, you know, to fall in and out of love with each passing season. I have never been in love before and never shall be again. As for marriage, I should always be comparing every other man with Ravenwilde and each would come up wanting. No, I shall simply live with my memories and be content to see him occasionally, for we are bound to meet."

"Yes, my love, we are bound to meet every morning over the breakfast table," came the laughing voice from the door.

Jumping up from the couch and turning so fast that she almost lost her balance, Sarah cried, "Ravenwilde! How long have you been there? You are the most bad-mannered man in all of England." Stomping one delicately shod foot she continued angrily, "From the very beginning you have made a habit of listening to my private conversations. How dare you, sir!"

Crossing the room and possessing himself of both her hands, which were now balled into tight fists, Ravenwilde said laughingly, "But, my dearest love, your *private* conversations are so much more informative than your *public* ones. I have been wondering this age how I could persuade you to marry me. Not until this moment did I suspect that you might be in love with me."

Jerking free, Sarah turned her back to him and said flatly, "I will not marry you."

"I should say not," Judith added smartly.

Ignoring Judith, Ravenwilde placed both hands on Sarah's rigid shoulders and asked softly, "And why not? You have admitted that you love me. Why will you not marry me?"

Turning to face him, Sarah replied angrily, "You! You, of all people, know my opinion of marriages of convenience, and you have the audacity to come here and ask me to marry you. Well, I shan't do it, Ravenwilde. I shall never marry without love." She was in a fine rage now, and seeing the amusement in his soft brown eyes made her even more angry. "Do not stand there laughing at me!" Please leave my house at once." Ignoring her own command, she continued, "You think you have to offer for me because of the little scandal and because of my injury. How dare you insult me thusly! Do you think I would stoop so low as to hold you honor bound to make a respectable woman of me? Little do you know of my character, sir! Now leave my house. And another thing," she continued as she paced the room, eyes flashing, "I am very well able to take care of myself. That is," she conceded, "with the help of my good friends. My friends, I might add, who stood by me while you raced off to God knows where. Now, leave my house. I never want to meet you again. And when we *do* meet, do not dare allude to any past events. Now, go."

"Did my leaving you in the care of my grandmother, who, incidentally, was far more capable of smoothing over the 'little scandal' than ever I could be, rankle so much, my love? You must know I did it for your own good. I knew matters would have been much worse for you if I were here to remind everyone that it was I who had led you astray. If you had but consented to see me before, I would have explained all that, and also that I had taken the opportunity to see your brother to ask him permission to seek your hand in marriage."

"My brother's permission, indeed!" Sarah stormed. "I, sir, am all of seven and twenty and have no need to ask permission of *anyone.*"

"Ah, yes," Ravenwilde replied with a hint of laughter in his voice. "I had forgotten your advanced age. It it weren't for my wretched memory, I probably would not be here now begging you to be my wife. What a man wants with such an *old* bride is past understanding, but there, I do want you, if you will but let me forget that you are practically an ape leader. Well, so long as you are not past the child-bearing age—for you know well that I want a *host* of children, unless, of course, they are born ugly, in which case we shall have to do with one or two—I shall suffer the stigma of your numerous years with equanimity."

Judith gasped, but for some moments now Sarah had been unable to control the twitch at the corners of her mouth, and when Ravenwilde heard the gurgle of laughter escape her throat, he advanced and took her tenderly into his arms.

"Don't you know, you silly goose, that I cannot live without you? I knew you had become necessary to my happiness, but I did not know how much I really loved you until I received that note from Donnelly telling me that he had you in his clutches. I died a thousand agonizing deaths before I could reach you. I wanted to rush to you at once, but I had to make plans for your ultimate rescue by sending a note to Oliver telling him what had happened and what I needed him to do. And after all my plans, you still almost got yourself killed."

"I am so sorry," Sarah answered, burying her face in the folds of his neckcloth. "How was I to know you had made plans for our rescue? I only knew I had gotten you into that awful mess and that I had to do something to ensure your safety."

"My safety would not have meant a thing to me if you had died." Tightening his hold on her, he said hoarsely, "I love you to distraction, my little darling. Please marry me. We can be at my grandmother's in time for Christmas if you will but say the word."

"For Christmas!" Sarah exclaimed as she pulled away from him a little in order to look into his beloved face. "We cannot possibly be married so quickly."

"Of course we can," he answered, releasing her in order to reach into his pocket for a document concealed there. "This, my only love, is a special license. I got it immediately after I talked with your brother. We can be married at once. Please say yes."

Judith came out of her shocked silence and said angrily, "She will do no such thing. Sarah, think what you are doing. You will dismiss this *person* at once and prepare to travel to the country with me. We shall leave at first light."

Barely taking note of Judith's outburst, Ravenwilde asked, "Is there someplace we can be alone?"

"Yes," Sarah answered dreamily as she led him to a small room adjoining the saloon.

As soon as the door closed on Judith's shrill voice, Ravenwilde took Sarah into his arms and kissed her soundly.

Looking into his teasing eyes, she said, "I do not know much about making love, sir. You will have to teach me."

Laughing softly, Ravenwilde proceeded to instruct her and was delighted to discover in her such a bright and willing pupil.

After a long session, Sarah asked breathlessly, "How many children did you say you wanted?" And much to the astonishment of the two ladies who were standing to hear the outcome of the lovers' private conversation through the closed door, there came the unmistakable sounds of laughter as Ravenwilde threw back his head and laughed until he collapsed into the arms of his willing Sarah.